SHATTERED:

A Family in Crisis

J. L. Coates

OTHER BOOKS BY THE AUTHOR

NON FICTION (Judith Coates)

Be Who You Be

Let Your Light Shine

THE ENLIGHTENMENT SERIES (J.L. Coates)

Second Chances

Awakening

Shattered: A Family in crisis

Copyright @2014

Library and Archives Canada Cataloguing in Publication Judith Coates

Judith Coates: e-mail: jcoates@telusplanet.net

ISBN 978-0-9880735-3-1

Printed in USA by CreateSpace

DEDICATION

THIS BOOK IS DEDICATED TO WARD, BRENDA, CHERYL, AND ALL FAMILIES WAGING A WAR AGAINST ADDICTION.

MY PRAYERS ARE WITH YOU.

CONTENTS

ACKNOWLEDGEMENTS

Thank you to my editor Dianne Tchir for doing another great job. Also thank you Clarice Nelson for your valuable input and helping me fill in the blanks. To my husband bob and my children, thank you for your love and continued support.

I wish to acknowledge that I borrowed the idea of the drop-in center from Stevie Cameron, author of "The Picton File" and "On the Farm – Robert Picton and the tragedy of Vancouver's Missing Women" published by Knopf Canada.

* * *

This story is near and dear to my heart. Although the names and places are fictitious the story is based upon a combination of true events and stories, some of which affected me personally.

I carefully researched various addiction support groups, and once again used a combination to support the story.

If you or a loved one is facing a battle with addiction I encourage you to contact and make use of resources available in your community.

I learned a very long time ago "we cannot fix others; the only person we fix is ourselves."

Love never gives up, never loses faith,

is always hopeful and endures through

all circumstances.

First chronicles 13:7

.

CHAPTER ONE

Emily Stuart's life revolved around her husband Ben and her daughter Jennifer. Everything she did was for them. Her main goal was to provide a home filled with calmness and serenity. It took much effort on her part to tolerate and ignore Ben's obvious distain for her.

Of course they had problems, but Emily chose to ignore them. The one that affected them the most was Ben's drinking. She insisted upon telling herself *I stopped worrying about that long ago. There is nothing wrong with Ben having a few drinks to unwind from his day when he gets home. He rarely has trouble getting up and going to work in the mornings, and only on the rare occasion have I had to call his office and tell them he was sick. He can handle his liquor. On those few occasions it was better for me to call his boss. That way they won't find out how much he really drinks. It's not like he has a drinking problem, or does it every week, he simply gets carried away every once in a while.*

When he wasn't drinking, Ben was the nicest guy one could want to be with. He was the same loving man she married. This helped compensate for the many arguments they had during the times he did drink too much.

Emily's daughter Jennifer, or Jenn they called her, was her pride and joy. At fifteen she was a caring young woman. She was an honor student; on the cheer leading squad and popular. There were always kids at the house or phoning her. Jenn was the perfect daughter, and this is what kept Emily from leaving when Ben was in one of his unpredictable moods.

Emily was in control of her life until the evening the insistent ringing of the front door bell woke her from her sound sleep. Through the open living room curtains, she could see the red and blue flashing lights of a police car parked in front of her house. The only other light in the room came from the flickering fifty inch television set.

Groggily she shook her head, and got up off the couch. Glancing around, she noticed Ben was not sleeping as usual in his brown leather reclining chair. She felt disorientated from being so sound asleep.

She didn't remember hearing Ben when he came home. Instead of waking her up he must have gone to bed. Each time he did this it, infuriated her. He knew how hard it was for her to get back to sleep, when she did go to bed after napping in the evenings. Usually, when he came home, he made enough noise to wake the dead.

She couldn't comprehend what was happening. Who would be ringing the doorbell this time of night? The abrupt awakening had added to the headache she already had. She always ended up with a headache after Ben was in one of his moods.

Stumbling to the door she opened it and saw two young police officers on the door step. Now she was fully awake. Her heart was pounding, and she could barely breathe. Had something happened to her daughter Jenn, or to Ben? Jenn had gone to the local high school football game with her friends, and then they were planning to go for Pizza afterwards. Forcing herself to be as calm as possible she said, "Hello officer is there something I can help you with?"

Taking off his hat, the one closest to her replied, "There has been an accident ma'am."

She gripped the door frame with her right hand to steady herself. She felt light headed, as though she was going to faint. "Is it my daughter Jenn? Has something happened to her?"

"No ma'am, it's your husband."

"Ben? What on earth has he done now?" Nothing he did surprised her anymore.

"There was an accident tonight on the corner of One sixteen Street and Carlton Avenue. Your husband was involved."

Emily felt sick. "Is he hurt?" she inquired.

"Ma'am, he was speeding, ran the stop sign on the corner, and hit another car broad side. That car was full of kids going home from the football game."

She collapsed against the door frame, nearly falling. her face a pasty white color. The young officer caught her, took her by the elbow, and guided her to the closest chair. She sat down heavily.

"Tell me what happened," she asked trembling. The room was spinning, and she couldn't catch her breath.

"Like I said, ma'am, your husband was speeding, drove through a stop sign, and ran into the side of another vehicle coming down the hill. There were five kids in the car, two were killed, three were seriously injured and one child is in critical condition"

"And Ben, what happened to him?" she asked, mentally

preparing herself for the worst possible news.

"He left the scene of the accident. He was found half an hour later walking down Carlton Avenue, about a mile from the accident, carrying a grocery bag in his hand. He appeared to be intoxicated. He told the apprehending officer he was on his way home to have a drink. I don't know for sure if he even realized he had been in an accident. He consented to a road side Breathalyzer, and was well over the legal limit. We immediately took him into custody for suspected impaired driving."

"How do you know it was him, or if he was the one involved?"

"There were witness's ma'am. One followed him until the police arrived."

"Where is Ben now?"

"He is being checked out at the hospital because he has a nasty gash on his forehead. When the hospital releases him we will take him to the local police detachment, and book him on several charges; the first being leaving the scene of an accident."

She looked up at the young officer and softly asked, "What do I do now?"

"There is nothing you can do tonight ma'am. I suggest, in the morning, you find him a good lawyer. He is going to need one." Then, in a caring voice he asked "is there anyone I can call for you? I know this must be quite a shock."

'No," she replied, "I will be fine. My daughter will be home soon."

The two policemen let themselves out. She sat on the chair until the reflection of the blue flashing lights disappeared from the window. Then, in a state of sheer panic, she ran upstairs to see if Ben was in bed. But he wasn't. She ran back downstairs and out to the brick patio by the pool, but there was no sign of him. Sometimes when he was drinking, he would sit out there and brood. Then she ran back through the house and out the front door, to see if his car was parked in the driveway. She was praying the police officer was wrong, but she had to make sure for herself that Ben wasn't home.

Oh Lord, she muttered aloud, *this can't be true. I have to find Jenn before someone tells her, but I don't know where she is.*

Back inside the house, she picked up her cell phone and dialed her daughter's number, but it went straight to voicemail. Walking back to the black leather couch she sat down with her head in her hands. She was shaking and in shock.

She flashed back to the argument Ben and she had earlier in the evening *I should have stopped him,* she moaned. *This is my fault. I should have taken his keys away from him, instead of letting him walk out the door. I knew he had too much to drink already, but I was too tired to fight with him again.*

She had waited supper for him, and as usual, he was late. When he finally did arrive home, she could see that he had been drinking. She was loading the dish washer when he came in to the kitchen. Instead of speaking to her, he opened and then slammed shut the cupboard doors.

"How come you're so late?" she asked. "Supper was ready an hour ago."

"Stopped at Tony's with the boys, since when is that a crime?" he replied.

As usual his abrupt answer put her on the defensive. *Whatever you say*, she muttered under her breath while dishing up two plates at the stove.

"I don't know why I even bother making supper. You're stopping to have a drink with the boys is becoming a bad habit, and I don't like it. I get tired of holding supper for you until you get home every evening. From now on Jenn and I are going to eat, and you can find something when you get here" They ate in silence in front of the television.

When she finished her meal she got up and went into the kitchen. There were a few pots that still needed washing. He followed her, leaving his dirty plate on the coffee table.

"Go back and get your plate and bring it here. I am getting tired of having to pick up behind you all the time." As usual he ignored her.

"Where's Jenn tonight?" he asked sarcastically, as he stood looking in the open door of the fridge. "That girl is never here."

"She went to the football game. You know the cheer leaders go to every game in town."

"That girl is nothing but trouble. She is either out running around or has her noisy obnoxious friends over in that pool you wanted. With all of that squealing and hollering, it's impossible to get to sleep. Why can't they go someplace else and carry on like that? You mark my words, she is going to get into trouble one day, and it will be your fault."

She bit back her angry retort. *How would Ben know if they were noisy? He was usually fast asleep in his rocker with a drink in his hand before ten o'clock. I'm glad Jenn brings her friend's home. This way I know where she is and who she is with. I'm doing my best to make sure she has the childhood I never got to have. I wasn't much older than Jenn when Ben and I got married and I don't want her doing the same thing."*

"What are you looking for?" Emily asked, as he slammed the fridge door shut, went into the pantry, and started banging things around.

"Orange juice."

"There's some in the fridge. You were looking right at it."

For some reason, Ben had recently switched from drinking beer to vodka when he got home from work. It made him angrier than he used to be. When he was drinking beer he was mellow, but now he always seemed to have a chip on his shoulder and looked for something to blame her for.

He went back to the fridge, stood and looked into the open door again. "What is this garbage?" he said, pulling out the open container, turning it upside down and dumping it on the floor. "You know I want Pacific O J and nothing else."

"This was on sale and is a lot cheaper," she replied, getting down on her hands and knees to sop up the juice with paper towel. "There was no reason for you to do this. What do you think you are trying to prove?" she said through clenched teeth.

"Can't you get it straight? If I tell you to buy Pacific O J, that's what I want. Can't you get that into that thick head of yours?"

Getting back on to her feet, and putting the dripping paper towels into the garbage can she replied icily, "If it's that important, I will go to the store and get you some as soon as I finish here. Ben, just for one night can't you drink what is here?

19

I'll stop tomorrow at the super market after work and buy some for you."

He turned and walked out of the kitchen swearing and cussing. The next sound Emily heard was the jingle of his car keys.

"Where are you going?"

"To the store, where do you think?" he answered belligerently. "It seems that if I want something done right around here I have to do it myself. I don't know why you can't get things right the first time."

"Give me your keys," she replied, "I'll go right now. You are in no shape to be driving."

"There is nothing wrong with me," he snapped. "You are always telling me I drink too much. Just for once shut up about it. If you weren't so tight assed, you would have a drink with me, let your hair down, and have some fun for a change. But no, you have to be prissy and perfect all of the time. Everything has to be done by the book."

Emily watched out the kitchen window as he drove away. Even though she was used to his name calling and angry outbursts tonight he had gone too far. *How could I do something so stupid as to buy the wrong kind of juice? I know how fussy he is, but I was just trying to save a few dollars. We never seem to have enough money. I should know better to than to try and talk sense into him when he has been drinking. It's just asking for a fight.*

She bent down and wiped up the sticky juice spot on the floor with a damp dish cloth, finished loading the dish washer, and turned off the kitchen light. She was tired. It had been a long hard week at work. *I know Ben is also under a lot of stress too with the new program coming on line at work. He will get over it. I, for one, will be happy when they finally get that stupid program up and running. Maybe then life will get back to normal."* She laid down on the couch, turned on the television, and promptly fell asleep

Now she was fully awake. She sat on the edge of the couch wondering what to do and where to find Jenn. Then the front door flew open, and her daughter ran into the house, sobbing hysterically.

"Mom, have you heard what happened? Tommy Walker, the star quarter back of our team and his best friend, Jason Bruce were killed tonight in a car accident. Somebody T-boned them on Carlton Avenue, and then ran away. Everyone is saying the guy was drunk, ran the stop sign, then didn't have enough guts to stick around and see what he had done."

"Emily looked at her weeping daughter and asked herself *how am I going to tell her? This will break her heart. Damn you Ben Stuart, what a mess you and your drinking have left me to clean up this time.*

Taking a deep breath she stood up, walked over to her daughter, took her in her arms and held her until she stopped crying. Then taking her by the arm, Emily led her to the couch and sat down beside her.

"Jenn, I have something important to tell you."

"Mom, it's not fair. Tommy was the most popular guy in school. I can't believe this happened to him. He had a football scholarship for the fall."

"Jenn, listen to me. I know there was an accident tonight

because the police were here and told me. They believe your dad was the person driving the car that hit Tommy Walker."

"What? Dad? They said the guy was drunk, and that he walked away from the accident without a scratch. My dad wouldn't do something like that. He would hang around and try to help. You must be wrong."

"I'm not wrong Jenn. The police left here about an hour ago, after telling me what happened. Your dad is in police custody right now, and we can't go to see him until tomorrow."

"Why are you saying these things to me? My dad knows better than to drink and drive. He wouldn't do what you said. Stop lying to me." She wrenched her body away from Emily's arms and ran upstairs. Seconds later Emily heard Jenn's bedroom door slam shut.

Quietly Emily sat on the couch with her head in her hands. *How are we ever going to get through this* she wondered?

CHAPTER TWO

She was sixteen and pregnant when she and Ben were married. Her parents did their best to try and talk her out of it, but she went against their wishes and married Ben anyway.

Jennifer Elaine was born six months later. She had blond hair, with grey blue eyes like her father. She was the perfect baby, always happy, and never cried unless she was hungry.

Ben's dream was to finish high school and then go to technical school to learn about computers. Two months after Jenn was born, Emily went to work as a cashier at the local grocery store and supported Ben while he went to school. They fought a lot in the early days of their marriage. She worked all day, picked up the baby at the sitter's, made supper, and did all of her house work. Ben refused to help her. Most of the time he demanded as much, or more attention than the baby.

When Jenn was a year old Emily began night school, and when she told Ben her plans they had one of the bitterest fights of their marriage: "women don't need an education. They can't learn like a man, and besides they end up pregnant, and can't be relied on at the best of times." His words still stung and continued to haunt her. It took four years, but she finally graduated with a degree in Business Administration. Shortly after graduating she went to work for Fred Jensen at his insurance company. Now, she was his office manager overseeing the work of three secretaries in three different departments.

Ben went to school during the day, and demanded absolute peace and quiet while he was studying. On weekends he would party with his friends. In reality, she and Jenn led lonely lives. On the weekends, if he was home, he always had a beer in his hand. Any comment about his drinking would lead to another argument. Ben's favorite comment was "a fellow has the right relax after a hard week, and not have someone nattering at him all the time."

Ben graduated with honours, and was immediately offered a job as a programmer with Harvest Telecommunications. The pay was good, and that was when they had bought the house. She worked hard renovating and decorating to make it the perfect place for Ben and Jenn to come home to everyday.

At thirty three, Emily still looked the same as when she married at sixteen. Although still pretty, with flawless skin, large dark brown eyes and delicate features, she was never taught the secrets of how to make the most of her features. Her dark brown shaggy hair hung to the top of her shoulders. She knew she needed a good haircut, but as long as her hair wasn't hanging in her eyes, she didn't care. It wasn't so much she didn't care; it was more because she had given up. Every time she tried to change something about her appearance, Ben made fun of her. After a while she stopped trying.

Over time, Ben's drinking increased, and she began making excuses for him. She would phone the office when he had a bad hangover and tell them he was sick. She made sure he got up on time every morning. One night, when he was drunk he wrecked her car. She covered up for him by telling the police it was her fault. They had been fighting, and she had tried to grab the steering wheel.

After her car was wrecked she drove him to work every morning and picked him up every evening because he had to be at work before she did. If he went out with his friends, she stayed up so that she could pick him up and bring him home from the bar in the middle of the night. Those were the early years. Now he seemed to have a little more control over when and where he drank.

Thoughts invaded her mind about the number of times she had begged him to quit drinking. He often promised he would, but never made any kind of serious effort.

She recalled asking Jenn, when she was younger, why she stopped asking him to come to her recitals or school concerts. Jenn looked at her and replied, "Why bother, he won't come anyway."

As much as she wanted to, she wasn't going to be able to cover up for him this time. Like it or not, he was going to have to face the consequences of his actions. In her heart, Emily didn't believe he was capable of doing that. She usually managed to get him out of his messes, but this time was different. The seriousness of his actions, and the fact that the police were holding him in custody for hit and run, meant this was out her control, and that scared her more than anything.

Early the next morning, after tossing and turning all night, she sat at the kitchen table looking in the Yellow pages for the name of a lawyer. She wasn't sure what kind of lawyer to look for. Ben always put her down by saying "I always have to look after things because if something happened to me you wouldn't have a clue what to do."

After flipping through numerous pages Emily recognized the name Joe Green as one of the lawyers who worked through her office. She dialed the number, and was immediately connected to an answering machine.

"Mr. Green," she said, "This is Emily Stuart. You don't know me, but I desperately need your help. The police were here, and informed me that my husband was involved in that terrible accident last night. One of the officers told me to get him a good lawyer. I work for Fred Jensen's insurance company here in town, and I recognized your name as someone the office has previously done business with. Could you please phone me back at your earliest convenience?" Then she spelled out her name, and left her phone number.

Several hours later the phone rang. Jenn and her friends had been talking all morning, and Emily was beginning to wonder if the lawyer would be able to get through. She reminded Jenn several times "I am waiting for an important call," but that didn't seem to make a difference,

"Mrs. Stuart, this is Joe Green. How can I help you?"

"My husband Ben was involved in that accident last night, and the police told me to get him a lawyer, but I didn't know who to call. I recognized your name in the Yellow pages. Do you think you could help me? I don't know what to do."

"I'll tell you what. I'll make a couple of calls; see if he has been charged, and then get back to you."

Emily steeled herself and made the phone call she dreaded, letting Ben's family know. She was an only child and her parents had both passed away. Ben's parents were divorced. His mother lived across the country and his father was working overseas. Although their contact with their son was limited, they still deserved to know.

Emily was also very worried about her daughter. Jennifer had gone out with some of her friends. When she returned home she was extremely upset, and was in her room crying. Every time Emily went upstairs to try and talk to her, Jenn would scream "Go away. Leave me alone," through the closed door.

Finally, after what seemed hours later, Joe Green phoned back. "Mrs. Stuart, Joe Green here. Your husband has been charged with some very serious offences. He will go to court on Tuesday morning to deliver his plea, and then it will be up to the judge whether he grants bail or not. I will take his case, but I require a ten thousand dollar retainer up front, and delivered to my office on Monday. Do you own your home?"

"Yes."

"Good. We will probably have to use that as collateral for his bail. "

"Do you need to have the full ten thousand on Monday?"

Emily was in a panic. *Where am I going to get this kind of money by Monday? We both have good jobs, but for some reason we don't have any savings. I will have to find a way. I can't stand the thought of Ben being in jail any longer than he has to be. There is no way of knowing when his actual trial will be. It could easily be months from now.*

"I will take half now, and the rest by the end of the week. I'll let you know if, and when more is going to be required. His bail hearing is scheduled for ten o'clock Tuesday morning. Can you be there?"

"Yes, but first I will have to phone my boss. I'm sure he will give me the day off."

"Mrs. Stuart, we will do the best we can for your husband, but it's not looking good. For now we have to wait and see what happens. Meet me at the court house at nine-thirty Tuesday morning. I will explain the procedures to you and what we are going to do."

"I don't want him staying there much longer. He needs to come home."

"We will talk about this on Tuesday okay? Right now I am going to the jail to get his version of the events that evening. It is important to know his side of the story,"

Emily and Jenn arrived at the court house slightly after nine. Neither one of them had slept the night before. A clerk directed them to court room 2B, and they sat on the bench outside the door until a very tall distinguished man walked up to them.

"Mrs. Stuart? I am Joe Green, your husband's attorney. Now listen closely. This is what we are going to try to accomplish today. Best case scenario is that he will be released until his trial, but on very strict conditions. Worst case - he will have to stay in jail until his trial begins. My guess is he will most likely be released on bail, but if he breaches any of the conditions, he will be returned to jail to await his trial. Do you both understand how serious this is?"

Emily nodded. "Yes, I do, but I'm not the one you have to make understand. Ben has always had a mind of his own, and often he only hears what he wants to hear. He is always trying to figure out what is going to be best for him."

At quarter to ten the court room door opened and they went inside to wait. Ben's case was number three on the docket

Emily was shocked when her husband walked into the court

room. He was still dressed in the same clothes as that night. Rumpled and dirty looking, he needed a shave, his eyes were red, and he was visibly trembling. It was obvious to Emily he was sick.

She turned to Joe Green and asked, "Has he seen a doctor? He looks awful."

"Mrs. Stuart, what you are seeing is a man who hasn't had a drink for several days and needs one very badly. A doctor checked him last night, and is keeping an eye on his condition. Within a day or two he should start to look and feel better. People who are used to drinking every day have a very difficult time when they are forced to stop abruptly."

Emily wasn't convinced, but there was nothing she could do about the situation right now. *That only happens to alcoholics, and Ben isn't one of those.*

Ben was charged with impaired driving, leaving the scene of an accident, two counts of dangerous driving causing death, and three counts of dangerous driving causing bodily harm. If he was found guilty, he would be going to jail for a very long time. Joe Green was hoping he could get the charges reduced. Instead of being quiet, Ben was combative. Emily wasn't surprised, he was always defensive when he was caught doing something wrong.

"Mr. Stuart you are charged with some very serious offences. How do you plead?" asked the Judge.

Ben jumped to his feet, and defiantly proclaimed "Your Honour, this is all a big mistake. This is not my fault. The driver of the other car was going too fast and cut me off as I entered the intersection. I tried not to hit him, but there was nothing I could do. I had no choice. They were speeding, and being kids, probably not paying attention. They should have been looking to see where I was."

"I am not here to debate with you Mr. Stuart, how do you plead, guilty or not guilty?

Joe green jumped to his feet and replied "Not guilty your Honour."

Ben turned on him. "Who do you think you are? I can speak for myself. I am telling you, this is not my fault. These charges are B. S. and everybody knows that. They are just looking for someone to blame, and I am it."

Joe Green reached up and dragged Ben back to his chair.

"You take your hands off me," Ben sneered at him. "Don't touch me again."

"Mr. Green, restrain your client or I will have him taken out of the court room. For the last time, how does he plead?"

Joe Green stood and faced the judge. "Not guilty. Your Honour, at this time I request Mr. Stuart be released on bail in the custody of his wife."

"Does the prosecution object?"

"Yes, we do. If he is released we believe that Mr. Stuart will continue drinking and driving, and continue to be a danger to this community. We intend to prosecute him to the full extent of the law, He was driving drunk; two young lads are dead, and we feel he should remain in custody until his trial"

"Mr. Green, do you have something you wish to say?"

"Yes, your Honour. My client has never been in trouble in the past. He is a good citizen of this community. He owns a home here, which leads me to believe that he is not at risk of fleeing the community or this court's jurisdiction. Also, his employer has told me that he is working on a difficult project, and it is essential that he be able to continue."

This argument was decisive enough to sway the judge. "Mr. Stuart I am releasing you on two hundred and fifty thousand dollars bail. As well, you are forbidden to drive until your guilt or innocence has been determined. You are to refrain from consuming alcohol, and are to report weekly for mandatory counselling for your addiction. In addition, you are not allowed out of your home between the hours of nine p.m. and seven a.m., unless it is a dire emergency, and your wife accompanies you. Lastly, you are forbidden to have contact with the families whose children were involved in this accident. If you fail to live within these conditions you will be remanded to police custody until your trial. Do you understand this?" he stressed.

"Also Mr. Stuart," he continued, "do yourself a favor and change your attitude. The type of behavior you have displayed in this court room will only get you into more trouble."

Ben jumped to his feet. "You can't tell me what to do. This is not fair. The accident was not my fault. I thought it was written in the Constitution that a person is innocent until proven guilty? If you will stop and listen to me, I can explain all of this."

"Mr. Green, I suggest that you make your client sit down, and keep his remarks to himself before I change my mind."

Joe grabbed Ben's arm, and once again, forcefully pulled him back on to his chair. "Ben, if you know what is good for you, you will shut up right now."

"This court is remanded until March 1 for trial. Next case," said the judge.

A guard stepped forward to take Ben back to his cell. When he touched his elbow, Ben jerked his body away and glared at him.

Outside the court room, Joe stopped and talked with Emily and Jenn, advising them about what they needed to do to arrange Ben's bail. Emily was crying. Jenn was stone faced.

CHAPTER THREE

Emily was shocked by Ben's behavior. For the first time, since they were married, she saw him for what he was. He had no regard for other people's feelings, nor was he able to accept responsibility for his actions. It was all about him, and always the other person's fault.

Then her feelings turned to disgust. He had made a spectacle of himself in front of the court, and in front of his daughter. Many of the people who were in court that morning, would assume he didn't care about what he had done. For the first time, she realized that he sincerely believed he had done nothing wrong.

After leaving the court house she took Jenn to school, and then went to the bank to withdraw five thousand dollars from Jenn's college fund which she had been saving since she was three months old. Holding the money in her hand she knew she wouldn't be able to pay it back before Jenn left for college, but this was the only choice she had.

Next, she delivered the money to Joe Green's office, and then returned to the bank to sign the necessary papers that allowed her to use their home as collateral for Ben's bail. It was late by the time she finished. Exhausted and angry, she decided to wait until the next morning to go and get him. All she craved was a little peace and quiet.

His attitude had shocked her. How could he honestly believe

what he was saying? Tonight she needed to spend time with Jenn, and help her make sense of everything that was going on. She wondered how she was going to help Jenn understand all of this when she didn't herself.

The next morning it seemed to take forever to get all of the paper work done. By the time Ben was finally released he was angry. "What took you so long?" He demanded. Emily said nothing.

They drove home in silence. When he walked into the house the first thing Ben did was go to the refrigerator, get a can of beer and gulp half of it down.

"Man that tasted good," he said. Taking a second can he added, "I need a shower to wash the stink of that jail cell off me."

Crap. I meant to take that out of the fridge before he got home. How can he walk in and do this after all that has happened. He knows that one of his bail conditions is no alcohol. Yet he is on his second can of beer, and hasn't been home for ten minutes.

Emily sat at the kitchen table, patiently watching him guzzle. "Ben, we need to talk," she said.

"There is nothing to talk about. You heard me tell the judge this was not my fault."

"Ben, two boys are dead; another is paralyzed from the waist down. How can you believe that?"

"Do I need to repeat what I said? You heard me tell the judge that the accident wasn't my fault, what else is there for you to know?"

"You drove through a stop sign and ran into them."

"No Emily, they drove in front of me. They had a yield sign and were supposed to stop when they saw me coming. That kid was driving too fast and not paying attention to what he was doing."

"How can you say that?" she screamed at him. "You had been drinking before you came home, and had a couple more during supper. I asked you not to go. I said I would get you the kind of juice you wanted in the morning. I even volunteered to go to the store for you. Do you remember that? But no, you had to be stubborn and go anyway. There are witnesses who saw what happened and watched you walk away. What were you thinking? Do you have any idea how this is going to affect us and your daughter? Now look at the mess we are in. I had to dip into Jenn's college fund to pay the lawyer just to take your case."

Ben looked at her quietly for a few seconds, and then said "this is your fault you know."

"My fault?" How can you say that? I had nothing to do with the accident. I wasn't even there." Emily replied, stunned by the accusation.

"If you had bought the right kind of orange juice like I told you to, none of this would have happened. I wouldn't have had to go to the store."

Emily looked at him with contempt. She couldn't believe he was shifting the blame to her. "You can't blame me. That's not fair."

CHAPTER FOUR

The next weeks were like living a nightmare. The media was unrelenting in their coverage. News of the accident had been picked up nationally, and Ben became the poster boy for drunk driving. It hurt to hear him described as a drunk, and referred to as some kind of uncaring monster. The media made it sound like he deliberately went out that night to hurt those kids. Every aspect of their life was public knowledge, and there was no privacy for any of them. Jenn went to both funerals, and was mixed up and confused. She refused to look at her dad or talk to him. Late at night, Emily could hear her crying in her room.

Emily knew that Ben probably drank way more than he should, and had for a long time, but he worked hard and loved life. She kept telling herself that he wasn't the only person in the world who ever made an error in judgment. She also tried, unsuccessfully, to convince herself that the accident was an act of fate - they all happened to be in the wrong place at the wrong time.

After the accident Emily became acutely aware of how intolerant people were; people she and Ben had known for years, people they included in their close circle of friends all turned against them. She was especially hurt the day Suzanne, her best friend, had taken her aside and said "Emily, Rob and I can't get mixed up in this. We all knew that Ben drank too much, and that one day something like this was going to happen. For now, we think it is better not to be seen with you in public, but if there is anything I can do for you, don't hesitate to call. Rob is up for a promotion and we don't want anything to jeopardize that. He has worked hard and deserves it."

What a hypocrite, Suzanne and Rob had been over to their house off and on for years. When Suzanne was sick, I went out of my way to help her. Guess you get to know who your real friends are when something like this happens, Emily thought.

She also began to notice the little things; the clerk in the grocery store who glared at her and said nothing, people who averted their eyes when they passed each other on the street, and then there were those who were downright rude. Many of them were people she had known all her life.

After a while, it became easier to look down at the ground when she did her errands around town. When she was unsure of the reception she would receive, it became easier to wait for the other person to speak. At work, she learned to ignore the glares and innuendos from the customers.

If I am being treated like a pariah I wonder what Jenn is going through?

One evening, while she was making supper, and Jenn was sitting on a kitchen stool watching her, she asked, "how is school going?"

"Fine."

"Just fine, Jenn?"I noticed that Sally and Mandy, and some of your other friends haven't been coming over. Would you like to invite them over for a barbecue and swim on Saturday?"

"They are too busy," Jenn replied. "Besides they won't come

anyway"

Emily could see the hurt and confusion in her daughter's face. She walked around the counter and gave her a kiss on the top of her head. "It will get better," she said reassuringly. "Do you want to talk about it?"

"No not tonight. Mom, why did this have to happen?"

"I don't know baby, I just don't know."

The next day at work, she got a real feel for what was being said in the community. She didn't mean to eavesdrop, but as she was coming down the hall with a fresh cup of coffee in her hand, she heard arguing coming from behind her boss's office door.

"I thought you would have fired her by now," a male voice stated.

"Are you serious? Emily hasn't done anything wrong, besides she is the best worker I have in this office. I would be lost without her," her boss replied.

"Well, you need to know that people are talking. They are wondering why she is still working here. If you don't get rid of her some are threatening to pull their insurance policies out of here. That husband of hers was drunk and killed two of our star athletes, or have you forgotten that?'

"Exactly why have you come here Joe?" Fred Jenson, Emily's boss, demanded. "If you got something you want to say to me, spit it out. Quit beating around the bush."

"It's just that I happen to agree with them. If she is going to continue working here I'm pulling my insurance from you, effective today."

There were a few mumbled words she didn't catch, and then her boss exploded. "Don't you dare threaten me! If that's how you feel, take your policy and shove it. Get the hell out of here. I don't need your business that bad. Neither you nor anybody else in this town is going to tell me who I can have working in my office. As far as I am concerned, this is none of your business."

She quickly returned to her desk, hoping that nobody had seen her eavesdropping in the hallway. Tears stung her eyes; she was shaking like a leaf. Up until now she hadn't realized how emotional the local people were, and how much hate was being directed at her.

Before leaving for home that evening, she went into her boss's office. "I overheard the exchange between you and Joe Turner this morning. I don't want the fact that I work here affecting your business. I will leave."

"Emily Stuart, you get that out of your head right now. You are not going any place. Nobody in this town is going to tell me how I should handle my business. To hell with them! I need you here- without you, this place will fall apart. I know this isn't easy for you or Jenn, but hang in there. Soon they will find something or someone else to talk about, and this will be old news."

"Thanks Fred, I needed to hear you say that. Thank you for standing up for me."

"Go home and spend time with your daughter," he replied brusquely.

They never discussed this again, but over the next few weeks more than a dozen clients phoned to cancel their policies. Some were probably legitimate cancellations, but she couldn't help wondering how many were because she was still working there.

Ben's trial date was set nine months after the accident and the closer it came, the more he drank. He barely left the house, and his company had put him on an unpaid leave of absence until the trial was over. Just as well, because most days he wasn't in shape to go to work anyway. He was impossible to live with, and no matter how much she tried to get him to listen to her, he refused. Each day became harder for her and Jenn to get through. They never knew what was going to cause him to start screaming and threatening them.

Joe Green was also fed up with Ben's antics and ready to walk away from the case. "Emily," he told her one day, "Ben has to stop his drinking. If anybody reports him he will be in jail so fast he won't know what hit him. One of the primary conditions of his bail was that he attends counselling for his alcohol addiction. According to my reports he went once, and never went again. If the judge had followed up his bail would have been revoked. See if you can get him to come in on Friday, sober. We really need to discuss his case, because we are running out of time."

Emily was able to get Ben to Joe's office in reasonably decent shape, but Joe was furious with both of them. "How do you think this is going to look when it comes to court," he screamed at them. "Emily, you were given the responsibility to make sure he stopped drinking and showed up for counselling. You should have come to me and been honest about telling me how much Ben was drinking."

Emily glared back at him, "don't you dare put the blame for this on me. I tried and tried, and besides, you're not the one who has to live with him. That hasn't been much of a picnic either."

"Can't you both see that the people in this town and the court are going to see his actions as having no remorse about the accident?"

"I know that," she replied bitterly, "but if they really stopped and thought about it, they would realize he is drinking more because he is feeling guilty. It wasn't like he purposely set out to kill those kids. It was an accident."

"Emily, what you have to realize is that the minute he got behind the wheel of his car in a drunken state, he put every person in danger that he met on the road that night, including himself. Can't either of you understand that? Stop defending him. Two kids are dead, one will never walk again. That," he said to Ben, who was swaying on his feet doing his best to stand up, "is what caused all of your lives to change. Take him home and try to get him in half decent shape for the trial," he snarled.

Emily turned and looked at Joe, "this is not my fault, and I don't understand why you and everyone else in this town blame me. There is no way I can sit with him all day, watching over what he is doing. I have to work so we can pay the bills and pay you. I can't do everything or be everywhere."

After they left, Joe Green was sorry for what he said. He came down on her too hard. Ben was the one who had to accept responsibility for what he had done, but as far as he was concerned, Ben Stuart was a complete idiot, and he didn't know how he was going to defend against that.

Emily dropped Ben off at home and drove back to work. Fred had been excellent about allowing her to take all the time she needed off work, but she didn't want it to look like she was taking advantage of him. The other girls in the office already thought he was playing favorites. One morning, she heard them discussing this in the coffee room, and the fact that they couldn't understand why she was still working there. She wanted to say something to them, to let them know, in no uncertain terms, that this was none of their business but, she was too tired to fight.

That evening, after they finished supper, she went into the living room where Ben was sitting in his chair with a drink in his hand, staring at the television.

"Ben, Joe says you have to stop drinking - at least until the trial is over. I think it will go better for you if you did."

"You both seem to think I have a problem. I can quit any time I want to. Besides, who gives a damn what other people think?"

"Ben you have a problem, and I don't think you realize how serious it is. You are destroying your life and ours. There is a very real possibility you are going to end up in jail."

"Get off my back Emily. You two are the only ones who think I drink too much, and as usual, you are blowing everything out of proportion. The only reason I hit that car was because it was speeding. They should have slowed down when they saw me coming. I have told you a million times, that this accident was not my fault. Now leave me alone."

"Ben, you drove through a stop sign. You are the one who is in the wrong. Can't you see that? For once in your life, you have to face the truth. You are responsible for this accident, and what happened to those kids. Like it or not, the time has come for you to face up to the facts."

One bitter word led to another. They stood there swearing and screaming at each other. Jennifer ran into the room crying. "Stop both of you. All you ever do these days is fight. I hate you both," and then she ran upstairs to her room.

Later, before she wearily crawled into bed, Emily knocked on Jenn's door. She knew she was still awake because the lights were on, and she could hear her daughter talking to someone on the phone.

"Jenn let me in please. I'm sorry you had to hear all of that."

"Not tonight mom. Just go away and leave me alone."

Emily turned, went into their bedroom and crawled into bed. When she left for work in the morning Ben was still sleeping in his chair.

CHAPTER FIVE

The date of Ben's trial crept up faster than Emily expected. They had reached an uneasy truce with Joe. She had to give Ben some credit, he did cut down on the amount he was drinking, and each time they met with Joe he was sober. She prayed that it wasn't too little too late.

His trial was scheduled to last for two weeks, and she attended every day to show Ben she supported him, but, in her heart, she felt it was a useless gesture. He didn't seem to care if she was there or not. She didn't want Jenn to come with her, but Jenn insisted. The court room was packed every day, not only with television and news reporters, but people from out of town.

Across the street from the court house, people marched up and down carrying signs - "He deserves to die too! Don't drink and drive! Booze kills!" Every one of them tore at her heart. Many of the sign carriers were from out of town, and the private interest groups were turning the trial into a circus.

Watching the picketers' parade up and down the street made Emily livid. *I don't understand why these people don't just go away, let the law do its job, and allow the families to handle their grief privately. So many people are hurting, including Jenn and I. What are they trying to prove? It is a little too late for that already. The deep scars for the families connected to this tragedy are going to last a lifetime.*

Although Joe Green did his best, the evidence against Ben was overwhelming. Ben's co-workers testified that Ben had been drinking heavily that evening, probably more so than usual. The bartender testified that Ben had been there for more than three hours, but couldn't say for sure how many drinks he had served him.

When asked, the convenience store worker pointed Ben out as the intoxicated man who came into his store and argued with him over the price of a container of orange juice. He told the court that Ben slurred his words, staggered, and knocked things over. He also stated that he finally had to ask Ben to leave or else he was going to call the police. He said Ben got into his car, and drove away leaving skid marks on the pavement. The stop sign in question was less than half a block from his store. He didn't see the actual accident happen, but heard the crash, and phoned 9-1-1 for help. Video surveillance tapes played in the court room confirmed his statement.

During his testimony, Ben stood up and tried to argue with the witness, but Joe yanked him, none too gently, back into his seat. Other witnesses testified that they had seen Ben walk away from the accident. After that, the last witness, a police officer, testified that when they first located Ben he was staggering down the middle of the road, carrying a grocery bag that contained a liter of orange juice.. A sobriety test done with the road side Breathalyzer indicated he was twice the legal limit for alcohol. A blood alcohol test, taken at the hospital, confirmed this finding.

The evidence against him clearly indicated Ben was guilty. Ben had chosen trial by judge alone, thinking that one person would understand him better than twelve. When they returned two weeks later to hear the Judge's decision Emily wasn't the least bit surprised that he was found guilty. Ben's face turned white and he staggered, nearly falling when the judge pronounced him guilty on all counts. For the first time she realized that he honestly believed he did nothing wrong, and was sure he was going to go home a free man. He tried to wrestle with the court officers when they took him away, all the while screaming that he was innocent, that the accident wasn't his fault.

At the sentencing hearing, Emily sat beside Ben as he listened to the victim impact statements. He sat there quietly, staring straight ahead. Listening to what the friends and family members of the dead boys had to say, broke her heart. The young boy now paralyzed from the waist down, spoke about losing his best friends, as well as how his own life would be changed forever. In the end, the judge sentenced Ben to twenty-five years in jail with no chance of parole until he served ten years. He didn't look at her or Jenn as he was escorted away.

They were devastated. They both knew he would receive a jail sentence, but never dreamed it would be so long.

"Mom," Jenn said, "ten years before he can apply for parole. That is such a long time." Then, with tears streaming from her cheeks she asked "Why? Why did he do this to us?"

"I don't know what to tell you Jenn," Emily replied helplessly.

"I hate him. He had no right to tear us apart this way. I hope he rots in jail."

"Jenn don't talk like that. Your dad is a good man who has a drinking problem. He never meant for any of this to happen."

"Don't you dare stand there and defend him" Jenn screamed at her. "I hate both of you. You are no better than he is." Then she turned and ran away sobbing.

Emily watched her go and didn't try to stop her.

She waited in the lobby of the court house until Joe Green appeared. He had gone to talk to Ben before they took him back to jail.

"Ben wants to file an appeal immediately," Joe said to Emily.

"Do you think that would do any good? What would his chances of winning be?"

"Honestly Emily, I think he would lose. The judge could have sentenced him to life with no parole. This way, after ten years, he may get out and still have a chance for a life with you and Jenn. The real question becomes can you afford to keep on going? It would cost at least another fifty thousand or more."

"I have already used Jenn's college fund to pay for this. I don't know where I could find that kind of money."

"You and Jenn take the time to talk this over. You don't have to make a decision, today and we have one year to file an appeal."

Jenn was waiting for her when she got home. Over supper they discussed the trial and Ben's appeal. They decided to leave the situation the way it was for the time being. Emily could see how hurt and angry Jenn was and that alone made her decision much easier. Her priority now was Jenn; not getting Ben out of jail.

In hind sight, she wished that she and Jenn had gone for counselling when all of this started. If nothing else, they may have been better prepared to cope.

None of Jenn's friends came over anymore, but occasionally her friend Carla did phone. After several calls Jenn asked Emily to tell Carla she wasn't home when she called. Although Emily didn't approve of lying for her she agreed because she wanted to do what was best for her daughter.

Emily was also hurting too, but in a different way. The man she had been married to for more than sixteen years had disappeared from her life. In some ways she thought it would have been easier if he had also died that night. Now everything was a challenge including single parenting.

Ben had looked after everything from paying the bills, to dealing with the insurance company. She was finding it hard to do all of this and wished now that she hadn't allowed herself to be so dependent upon him.

Ben's phone calls from jail were the worst. Every day he phoned begging her to come and get him. Sometimes he was in tears, other times ranting and raving, calling her ugly names, and blaming her for the accident. He even went so far as accusing her and Joe Green of conspiring to get rid of him, so they could be together. He claimed he had proof they were lovers, and that was the real reason they weren't going ahead with his appeal. No matter how she tried to defend herself he wouldn't listen.

When he had called the last two times, she had answered the phone, placed it on the cupboard and went into the living room. She knew he was allowed five minutes, so just before his time was up, she went back to the phone, said her goodbye and hung up.

She nearly had all she could take. In the back of her mind she debated about getting a divorce. This wasn't what she wanted, but if he was going to continue harassing and verbally abusing her for the next ten years, she would lose her mind.

Several times he asked to speak to Jenn. After the second call Jenn was reluctant to talk to him. The next time he phoned, and with her daughter's consent, Emily listened to their conversation from the extension in the living room. She was shocked at the way he begged his daughter to intervene for him, and the ugly names he called her mother. The next time Jenn refused and Emily understood why.

After that call Emily decided she needed to talk with Jenn again. She explained more fully about using her college fund to pay for her father's defense, and the only way she could afford to pay for an appeal was to either sell the house, or take out a second mortgage. The evidence against him was so strong that not only would it be a waste of money, but that he could receive a longer jail sentence.

Jenn listened to her patiently and then said, "I trust you mom. I know you will do what is best for us."

One day, in a burst of anger she packed all of Ben's things into boxes, and then relegated the boxes to a back corner of the garage. She justified this by telling herself *it isn't so much that I want to get rid of Ben's things, it's just that they remind me too much of what Jenn and I have lost. Everything will be there if, and when, he needs them.*

Although there was still a great deal of hostility directed at them. Emily had also convinced herself that she and Jenn were making progress, For the most part; the town seemed to be moving on.

All of that changed when Jenn walked in the door after school, crying. Her blouse was torn, there were scratches on her cheek and hands, and one of her eyes was black and blue. Emily ran to her daughter's side and put her arms around her.

"My God Jenn, who did this to you?"

"Carla Perkins, and a bunch of her friends."

"Why? Carla has been your friend for years. She is the only one who has phoned to talk with you. What happened?"

"They were waiting for me outside of the school. Carla started calling me names. I asked her to stop, but she wouldn't, so I hit her. I couldn't take anymore of her taunting. Carla punched me in the face, and the next thing I knew we were wrestling on the ground. A bunch of kids gathered around, and were screaming at her to kick my ass. It was awful. Finally one of the teachers saw the fight; came over and stopped it. Mom, this goes on every day. All those times you thought Carla was phoning to be my friend; she was calling me names and making fun of me. Finally I had enough, and decided to fight back."

"If this was going on why didn't you tell me or someone, - like a teacher? Someone from the school could have talked to her and made her stop."

"I told the principal, but he didn't do anything. I don't even think he pulled her aside and talked to her. Maybe, in their own way, they agreed with her, I don't know."

"Baby, I am so sorry you had to go through this. I am going to the school in the morning to have a chat with that Principal," Emily replied indignantly.

"Mom, don't. All that will do is make things worse. I will be fine"

Emily hugged her daughter. Then she asked, "If you look this bad, how does Carla look?"

Jenn giggled, "Worse than I do."

CHAPTER SIX

Emily couldn't sleep. She spent most of the night thinking about what she should do. *Jenn is never going to have a chance if we stay here. She shouldn't have to put up with being bullied at school for something her father did. Nor should she have to put up with snide remarks or innuendo. If it is this hard for me to deal with, as an adult, it must be twice as hard on her. What probably makes it worse is that not long ago these were Jenn's best friends, and now they have turned on her. Neither one of us is responsible for what happened. People should realize that that our lives have been changed too, but I guess few people are willing to live and let live. Maybe I should divorce Ben, and then we can truly start over."*

The next morning, on her coffee break, Emily phoned Joe Green. Joe was no longer just her lawyer, but he and his wife had also become good friends.

"Hi Emily," he said, "What can I do for you today?"

"Do you have a minute?"

"Sure, you know I will always make time for you. What's up?"

"Joe, I have decided to file for a divorce from Ben. I was hoping over time that things would get better, but if anything, they are escalating for Jenn. She is having trouble in school."

"Are you sure this is what you want? It's a big step and there

53

is no going back."

"Joe, Ben is going to be in jail for ten years before he can even apply for a parole. My daughter is getting beat up and bullied at school. Her grades are failing. Fred has people cancelling their insurance policies because I work there. Looking into the future, I can't see this getting any better."

"Emily, do you think this is being fair to Ben?"

"He should have thought of that when he drove away from the house drunk," she said bitterly. "Besides ten years is a long time to hang on to a marriage that was in trouble in the first place. When I look back, this ending was inevitable."

"Okay if that's what you want, if you are absolutely sure."

"I am sure."

"I'll start the paper work today. You are aware that under the law, even if he is in jail, he is entitled to half of everything?"

"I don't care. Give him whatever he is entitled to. It won't do him any good where he is, but Jenn and I have to be able to move on with our lives."

"Personally," Joe replied, "I think you are making the right decision, but as a lawyer I have to ask these questions. I'll get back to you on this. What are your plans?"

"I have decided to sell the house and move away from here."

"Have you told Jenn?" What does she think about this?"

"I don't know, I only decided last night. I am sure she will be fine with it."

"You are aware you will be taking her away from her friends and school. That can be hard on someone her age. This commotion will eventually die down – there is no need to uproot your lives."

"Joe, it has been over a year since the accident happened and it's not getting better. I would stay if people would leave us alone and let us get on with our lives."

"Think this over more thoroughly Emily, but in the end it is your decision to make."

They chatted for a few more minutes, and then Emily hung up. Her next call was to the local real estate office. She listed her house for two hundred and twenty-five thousand dollars. If she got her price, Ben would have more than enough money to get started over again, when he got out of jail. She would have enough for a down payment on a house and still be able to put some back into Jenn's college fund.

At closing time that same day Emily knocked on her boss's office door and entered. "Fred, I want you to be the first to know that I am divorcing Ben, and have listed my house for sale. This is no place for us to be right now. Maybe in time people will stop blaming us, but, until then, it's getting harder and harder to live here. Jenn got beat up at school yesterday, and that was the final straw. I have to think of her well-being first.

"What are your plans?" Fred asked, looking up from the files on his desk.

"I don't have any yet."

"Emily I hate to lose you, but I understand what you are saying. This must be a difficult experience for both of you. Let me look into something. Sometimes other agents, within the company, are looking for good trained people to work for them. I'll see if there is any way I can arrange a transfer to another branch, and that way you get to keep your benefits."

"Fred, I really don't want to leave, but I feel I have no other choice. This is my home. I have lived here all of my life, but I have to think about what is best for Jenn."

Fred got up from behind his desk, went over to Emily and gave her a big hug. "You are right, but before you up and quit, let me see what I can do."

That evening when Jenn came home from school, they sat down to talk. "Jenn, I have been doing some serious thinking, and hopefully what I have decided will be best for both of us." I talked to Joe Green today and have started proceedings to divorce your dad. I have also put the house up for sale and Fred is going to try and find a transfer for me to another office. I think that moving away from here and starting over - just the two of us is a good idea."

Jenn started to cry. "Mom, why do we have to do this? Why can't people leave us alone and let us live our lives? I don't want to move away from here because of what they say and do. It's not fair."

"I know baby, I know," Emily replied, her eyes filling with tears. "Sometimes life isn't fair."

Within a couple of weeks her plans began to fall into place. Ben agreed to the divorce and asked for only what he was entitled to. The house sold quickly and the new owners agreed to let them stay until the end of the school term. Fred arranged for a transfer to a larger town named Jesse, located a hundred miles from where they lived now. They would still be close enough to family and friends to celebrate the holidays, but far enough away to start over.

It took a while, but after several house hunting trips, they found the perfect house. Moving was going to be a major adjustment for both of them. Packing up and leaving their home was the hardest part, every room had a memory. Every room held Emily's personal touch.

For a solid week she and Jenn packed what they were going to take with them. It was especially hard to let Ben's things go

Finally Jenn said to her, "this is taking too long. When he gets out of jail his clothes will be out of style anyway."

Emily was amazed at what she accumulated over the years, but finally, after donating, selling and filling numerous bins of garbage they were ready to go.

Eventually the day came when everything they were taking was in the moving van. On the way out of town, Emily stopped at the real estate office and dropped off the keys.

Jenn was quiet on the drive. "Mom we could have stayed here. I could have learned to ignore what the other kids were saying. Are you sure this is the right thing to do?"

Firmly Emily replied, "I hope so Jenn." As long as we are here, someone will be whispering behind our backs or pointing a finger at us. We need a fresh start. Maybe," she added wistfully, "maybe one day we will be able to move back."

"I hope so mom." Jenn replied.

They rode the rest of the way in silence, each wrapped up in their own thoughts.

CHAPTER SEVEN

The house they decided to purchase was an older two story home with a lot of character. There was a large fenced backyard, with a brick patio off the back deck which would be ideal for entertaining. There were flower beds along the fences, and in the middle of the yard was a fountain. Close to the fountain stood a huge maple tree with a black wrought iron bench tucked beneath the branches. Emily could picture herself, sitting there in the cool of the summer evenings reading a book and listening to the sound of the trickling water.

Flower beds filled with red and white flowers lined each side of the front sidewalk. The house had a front porch, two white wicker chairs, and wicker table that the previous owners, an older retired couple, wanted her to have.

In no time at all their goods were unpacked. Jenn claimed the upstairs bedroom, while Emily was content to have the larger bedroom on the lower floor. This arrangement gave them both a degree of privacy. She planned to make the second bedroom on the main floor into a game and television room for Jenn and her new friends.

The next weeks were hectic. Jenn settled well into her new school, but Emily's job at the insurance agency was challenging and busier than the office she left. On top of everything, they were in the middle of changing to a new computer system, and she had to become familiar with that.

One evening, while she was preparing supper for the two of them, Jenn wandered into the kitchen and sat down at the table. Emily could see she had been crying.

"What is the matter Jenn?" You look so sad."

"Mom, can we move back home?"

"Why? I thought you liked it here?'

"I hate it. The kids aren't friendly, and my teachers suck. Sometimes I think they don't care if we learn anything or not."

"It'll be okay Jenn." Give yourself time to make new friends. I am sure the teachers know what they are doing."

"Everybody thinks I'm a nerd."

"Why, because your grades are good?"

"No, because the teachers told everyone I was an honor student, and they were glad to have me in their classes. They said I would set a good example for the rest of the class."

"Jenn, you are a smart, beautiful, young lady. Once they get to know you, they will change their minds. The new kid in school usually finds it tough going for the first little while, but after a week or so things begin to change. I am finding the same thing in the office, but we will get through this."

"Please mom. I want to go back home and be with my friends. I really don't want to be here."

"Jenn, friends stick by each other. They don't treat you the way yours did."

"I know mom, but they would have eventually stopped."

"We can't right now Jenn. I honestly think it's better for us to be away from there for a year or so. There are still too many people angry about the accident. Perhaps, in time, they will stop blaming you and me. Until then, I think this is the best way. Do you think you could be more patient and try for just a little bit longer? I am sure things will get better."

"If you say so mom, I sure hope you are right."

After their conversation Jenn began to settle down. Her first report card put her back on the honor roll. She seemed happier and the phone was once again ringing for her. Occasionally she brought a few of her new friends' home. Emily breathed a sigh of relief. Now more than ever, she felt like she had made the right decision.

Her new job was time consuming, and they became like two ships passing in the night. The only time they were able to spend together was on weekends. Although Jenn didn't complain, she did make one or two remarks about Emily never being home to cook supper.

One evening before going to bed, Jenn stopped at Emily's bedroom door. "Mom I know you are busy, but you are never here. I miss sitting in the kitchen with you while you are making supper. You know, the way we used to. I miss dad too. I wish we could go back to the way it used to be." Then she was gone.

Emily lay there thinking for a long time. This wasn't how she wanted to raise her daughter, so she made a conscious decision to try and get home from work earlier to spend more time with her. The few evenings she did get home from work early, Jenn always had something going on. Most of the time, Emily was in bed when she heard her daughter come in.

Then she noticed that slowly and imperceptibly Jenn began to change. At first it was little things - like too much black eyeliner. Rather than voice her displeasure Emily put it down to a phase Jenn was going through. Probably all of the other girls at school were doing the same thing, and Jenn was merely trying to fit in.

Jenn became sullen and pouty. When she suggested they do something together, like going to a movie, Jenn rolled her eyes and walked away. She became aloof and uncommunicative. Emily missed the times they used to sit in the kitchen drinking hot chocolate and talking.

Also gone were the pretty bright colors she used to wear. Now everything she wore was black. She had always been particular about how she looked; now all of her clothes were too big and baggy,

The first indication she had that there was a problem was when Jenn's teacher phoned and asked her to come to the school. She mentioned that Jenn was missing a lot of classes and she was falling behind. Alarmed, Emily agreed to meet her that same afternoon.

"Mrs. Stuart, I am Jane Pomery," the teacher said extending her hand. In return Emily shook hands with her. "Please sit down. I am so glad that you have come"

Emily sat across the desk from her. "You mentioned Jenn has been missing a lot of classes. I don't understand what you mean."

"Yes she has, but that is not the main reason I asked to meet with you. When Jenn moved to our school she was a bright, smart, young lady. I read her school records and saw she was a cheer leader; active on her student council, as well as being an honor student.

"Yes, she was vice president of the student council."

"We understand that both of you lived through a very traumatic experience before coming here?"

"Yes. Jen's father was involved in an accident, and is now in jail. We divorced and I moved here with the idea of starting over- just the two of us. I didn't realize how mean some kids could be. The day she came home from school with a black eye, I decided we needed to move, and I was lucky enough to be able to get a transfer here."

"I am sorry to hear that. Some of the students have found out about this and are giving her a hard time. Do you think that could be the reason she doesn't come to school every day?'

Emily shrugged her shoulders. All of this was new to her, Jenn hadn't said a word. "I am having a problem with the fact that she is skipping school. That is so unlike her."

"Mrs. Stuart, there is a group of students in our school who call themselves the "misfits". Kids who, for whatever reason, are having difficulty fitting into the school environment. Over the past little while Jenn has gravitated to this group, and is taking on many of their mannerisms. I am concerned for her. I am sure you have seen some of these changes yourself.

"Yes, I have. I've just been giving her space. I thought she was going through a phase, and would get over it.

"Mrs. Stuart, it is rumored that there is rampant alcohol consumption within this group, and we have also heard rumors of drug abuse.

"My Jenn wouldn't get involved with that," Emily responded heatedly, "She has seen and experienced first-hand what too much drinking can do."

"Mrs. Stuart, I am not saying that is what Jenn is doing. I wanted to give you a heads up as to the type of kids she is hanging around with, and what direction she could be headed in. We have an excellent school counselling program here, and if you are interested, I could set up an appointment for you with the counsellor. With your permission I am sure we can get Jenn into the program."

"I'll have to think about that, now about Jenn missing school?"

"Yes, some days she doesn't come at all, other days she comes for a little while and then leaves. She usually stays long enough to be marked as attending. She is failing all of her classes and has been put on academic probation."

"What does that mean?"

"Until her grades improve to passing, she is not allowed to take part in any of our extracurricular activities."

Emily stood up to leave. She was shocked at what the teacher had told her. "This isn't like Jenn at all. I don't know what to say. I had no idea any of this was going on. I will have a talk with her and see if I can find out what is behind this behavior. Also, I will think about the counselling offer. Thank you for telling me all of this."

Emily felt sick to her stomach. The only hope Jenn had of going to college was to earn a full scholarship. She had replaced some, but not all of the money she used for Ben. Certainly it was only enough for one or two years.

"Mrs. Stuart, I strongly suggest that you meet with our counsellor and find out about the program. It is excellent. If we get started soon we may be able to stop the downward spiral your daughter could be getting caught up in. The misfits are bad news, and your daughter is extremely vulnerable right now."

"I have to think about this first," Emily replied.

Mrs. Pomery watched Emily walk down the hall. In her heart, she knew Emily was in denial and Jenn wouldn't receive the counselling she needed, and within a few months, would stop coming to school all together. She had seen this scenario played out a dozen times over the years, and it never ended well. Some parents couldn't accept the fact that their children had serious problems.

Emily waited up for Jenn to come home that evening. When she did get home, a little past ten, her eyes were red and bleary looking.

"Jenn, we need to talk."

"Now what?" she replied sarcastically.

"I had a meeting this afternoon with your teacher Mrs. Pomery. She told me you are skipping school; that your grades are failing, and that you are on academic probation."

Suddenly the old Jenn emerged. "Mom, I really hate it here. It's not my fault you know. Some of the kids are teasing me about dad being in jail. Please can we move back home?"

"Oh Jenn, I didn't know it was that bad. Mrs. Pomery suggested that you talk with the school counsellor. Apparently they have an excellent program here. Maybe that will help, you know, if you had someone to talk to. I could go with you."

"Mom, get serious. Do you have any idea how much more the kids would tease me if they found that out? No, thank you."

"Jenn, I will make you a deal. You go back to classes, get your grades up, and I will find a way to get you back into your old school next fall. How does that sound?"

"Sure mom that will be great." Jenn seemed to lose track of the conversation. Without saying anything more she turned, walked away, and went upstairs to her room.

Jenn's behavior struck Emily as odd. She had never done that before, maybe she wasn't feeling well. She looked like she was getting a cold.

Two days later, while running an errand downtown for her boss, Emily saw Jenn on the street with some of her friends. She should have been in school. Obviously she skipped again. Their little talk the other night had no effect on her. Emily felt uneasy seeing the way they were dressed and their swaggering attitude as they strutted down the street. They wouldn't move over at all, and anyone meeting them on the sidewalk had to step out into the busy road to get past. She and Jenn would be having another little chat this evening.

Once again she waited up for Jenn. When she walked in the door Emily could see and smell that she had been drinking.

"I saw you downtown when you should have been in school this morning. You promised me that you weren't going to skip anymore classes."

"So?"

"Look at me. Have you been drinking? I thought, after what we have been through with your dad, you would see what can happen and stay away from that stuff."

"Mom, shut up! Get off my back. Jenn do this, Jenn do that. Do you ever stop just once and think about what I want. You are doing the same thing with me that you used to do to daddy. Always running our lives, and always telling us what to do. I can hardly wait until I am eighteen so I can get out of here," her daughter screamed at her.

"Don't you dare talk to me like that," Emily screamed back. "You are my daughter. You are under age, and from now on you will follow the rules in this house. Number one is no drinking, number two is that you will go to school every day, and number three you will talk to me with respect." Emily counted off the rules on her fingers as she named them.

Jenn turned and staggered toward the stairs. Then she turned back and said, "You are a real bitch, do you know that?"

Not even thinking about what she was doing, Emily walked over to Jenn and slapped her across the face. Both of them were stunned by her sudden outburst of violence.

"Don't you ever call me that again," Emily snarled at her daughter.

Jenn looked at her eyes blazing and defiant. "Don't you ever touch me again," she snarled back over her shoulder as she started walking up the stairs.

Immediately overcome with remorse, Emily said "Jenn wait, I am sorry. Please come back, so we can talk about this."

Jenn ignored her mother and continued marching upstairs. Emily, feeling broken and bewildered, went into the living room and sat down on the couch.

Now what? What is going on in Jenn's life that is causing her to act out this way? Everything she is doing is completely out of character. None of this makes any sense. Maybe if I try a little harder, she will come around.

Briefly she thought of looking into the school counselling program, but shrugged it off. Jenn had already said she didn't want to go.

CHAPTER EIGHT

Over the next few days an uneasy truce developed between them. Jenn tried to be home earlier in the evenings, and spend more time with her mother. Emily was grateful for Jenn's efforts and did her best to be home to cook supper every evening, even if it was late. There were a lot of questions Emily wanted to ask Jenn, and many things she wanted to say, but she hesitated. She didn't want Jenn mad at her again.

This all ended two weeks later while Emily was sorting the laundry. By force of habit she always checked the pockets to make sure they were empty. One time she accidentally washed Ben's credit card and he was furious with her.

When she picked up Jenn's jeans to toss them into the washer a plastic bag filled with green leafy material fell out onto the floor. Her heart sank. Although she had never seen it before, she instinctively knew the substance was marijuana. That explained why Jenn's eyes looked so red and bleary at times. She was furious. She didn't know what to do, or what would be the best way to handle this new development. *This kid is driving me crazy. I don't know what to do with her anymore. Talking doesn't seem to help.*

All day she wondered, should she confront Jenn or should she simply throw it in the garbage, and pretend she never saw it? If she did decide to bring the issue up with Jenn she hoped they could sit down and reasonably discuss the pros and cons of using drugs.

When Jenn came home that evening, the first thing she saw in the middle of the kitchen table was the bag of marijuana. Emily said to her sadly, "I found this in your jeans pocket when I was doing your laundry."

"It's not mine mom, I was holding it for a friend."

"Jenn, don't lie to me. You and I both know what this is, and what is going on here. My question to you is why?"

"I don't know why mom. All the other kids are doing it and I want them to like me. I tried it because they dared me to, and I like the feeling it gives me."

Emily picked up the bag, walked over to the garbage disposal, turned it on and dumped the bag into it. "Young lady, you are grounded for the next month. Furthermore, I forbid you to hang around with those kids anymore. I will personally drive you to school and pick you up, and I am going to make an appointment with that counsellor at school. You are better than this."

"You can't make me do any of that. Do you even realize how much trouble I am in because of what you just did? I don't have to listen to you. I wasn't lying; I really was holding it for my friend."

"So, let your friends hold their own drugs. You know better than to bring that stuff into this house. I am your mother, and you will listen to me and do what I say"

"And if I don't?"

"Jenn, go to your room. I don't want to fight with you. This is the way it is going to be until you can prove that you can act and think responsibly."

Jenn glared at her mother, and replied sarcastically, "whatever," then stomped up the stairs again. In the morning she was gone and so were two hundred dollars and the credit cards Emily had in her purse.

CHAPTER NINE

Emily was frantic. *Where could she be? This is my fault. I was too hard on her last night I should have tried to reason with her, instead of getting angry. Over the past year our lives have gone to hell and I don't understand why. Jenn has never gone into my purse without permission, nor has she taken money without asking. This whole thing is not like her at all. I am sure that once she cools down she will come home. When I get home from work tonight I bet she will be waiting for me.*

Over and over she went through the previous evening's event, recalling every word and action. She tried to think how she could have handled the situation differently, but nothing came to mind. In many ways it was like dealing with Ben all over again, and she had messed that up too.

She felt like she was on pins and needles all day. She phoned home every hour, but there was no answer. She rushed home from work and waited. By eight o'clock she was beside herself. She picked up the phone and called the local police station."

"How may I help you?" a crisp friendly voice asked.

"I want to report that my daughter is missing," Emily replied.

"One moment please."

Seconds later a deep husky voice came on the line. "Detective Don Beatty, how can I help you?"

"My name is Emily Stuart and my daughter Jenn is gone."

"What do you mean by gone."

"I don't know where she is. She left sometime during the night and hasn't come home yet. She has never done anything like this before." With each word Emily's voice was rising hysterically.

"Calm down Mrs. Stuart, Take a deep breath, and tell me what happened."

A torrent of stored up words spilled from Emily's mouth. She told him about Ben's accident, his going to jail, why they had moved, and the many changes she had seen in her daughter. Then she told him about Jenn's drinking and finding drugs in her jeans.

Don Beatty sat there quietly and listened. He had heard this same story so often, and each time it bothered him. "Mrs. Stuart, we usually ask you to wait seventy two hours before you file a missing persons report. I'll tell you what, give me a description of your daughter and I will ask the patrol officers to watch out for her. If they see her, they will approach her and tell her to go home - that you are worried."

"Thank you. Jenn is about five feet one inch tall with long blonde hair, blue gray eyes, and weighs about one hundred pounds. She usually wears her hair in a ponytail. She is small for her age, sixteen years old and pretty. Please, I am so worried about her. Oh, and she will probably be dressed all in black, and have too much black eyeliner on. All she ever seems to wear is black clothes that look too big for her."

"Give me your phone number, and if I hear anything, I will

call you. I am sure everything will be all right, and she will come walking in the door like nothing happened and won't understand why you are so upset."

Despite his reassurances, Emily couldn't stay home. She got in her car and drove up and down the streets looking for her daughter. It was a real eye opener when she turned a corner and found herself in a seedy part of town that she never knew existed.

Four days passed and Emily still didn't hear from her daughter. She felt numb and had no idea who to turn to. Don Beatty hadn't called her back, so she assumed that probably meant that none of the patrol officers had come across her.

She was sitting on the back deck, drinking her morning coffee when she heard the front door bell ring. Not sure what to expect she dashed for the front door, but in her hurry stubbed her toe on the cupboard. Grimacing, she limped to the door and opened it. Jenn was standing there.

"Mom, can I come home?'

She didn't say anything. Taking her daughter into her arms she held her tight. "Thank heavens you are here. I have been frantic. Where have you been?"

"Mom I am really sick – leave me alone right now. We can talk later."

Emily stopped and took a long look at her daughter. Her hair was matted, her clothes were filthy, and she reeked of smoke, booze and sex. "Jenn, where have you been?'

"Please mom, All I want is a bath and to lie down for a while. I will tell you the whole story later."

"Go ahead. I'll make us some scrambled eggs – the way you like them."

"Mom," Jenn said sharply. "I'm not hungry, later okay?"

While Jenn was having a shower Emily phoned Don Beatty at the police station. She left a message, letting him know that her daughter was home and that she wanted to cancel the missing persons report.

Jenn slept for twenty four hours straight. Emily watched over her when she cried out in her sleep and thrashed around the bed. Emily was afraid for her. She debated about phoning a doctor but eventually Jenn settled down and slept peacefully. Emily slept in a chair beside her bed, barely leaving her side.

Finally Jenn awoke. Emily was downstairs making breakfast when she heard her padding down the steps in her bare feet.

"Oh, you're awake. Do you have any idea how long you slept? I was starting to get worried," Emily said.

Not knowing what else to do, she got busy at the stove, and within minutes dished out scrambled eggs and toast on a plate for each of them. Jenn ate a few bites and then started to cry.

"Something terrible happened mom, and I am so ashamed," Jenn stated quietly. "That night I ran away I went to the park where the kids from my school hang out. We hung out there drinking for a while, and then one of the guys suggested we go to Juniper Lake. He knew of a party at one of the cabins. When you go to those things you can't go empty handed, so I gave him the money I took from your purse. The boys knew where to buy some more beer and some drugs. Then we jumped into one of their cars and headed for the lake.

Everything seemed okay at first, I knew mostly everyone there, and we were having a good time until some other kids showed up. Then it got nasty. I tried to leave, but I couldn't find a ride home so I ended up going back into the cabin and joining the party. The boys forced me to stay there. I couldn't get away. They forced me to do drugs, and took turns using me for sex. I begged to go home, but they just laughed.

When they ran out of drugs they brought me as far as the edge of town and dropped me off at a house with one of their friends. When I explained what was going on and asked for help, he laughed at me. This guy named Skeeter was there, and he helped me get away. He brought me home. Mom, it was terrible. I didn't know what to do. The battery on my cell phone died, and I had no way of calling you."

Emily felt sick to her stomach. "We have to phone the police Jenn, and tell them what these people did to you."

"Mom, why don't we just forget it? If I go to the police and they find out, they said they would kill me. I'm scared. It's not such a big deal really."

"Jenn, it is a big deal and they must be stopped. What if they do this to other girls? What if one of them gave you a disease, or got you pregnant? Then what?"

"Mom I will handle this. I don't want to talk about it anymore, I am not going to the police, and neither are you. I want to forget this ever happened. If you say anything to anyone, I will leave again. I won't get pregnant, I'm on the pill."

"You are what?"

"I said I am on the pill, and have been for a long time. I'm not so stupid that I don't know how to look after myself. So let it go okay."

Jenn was anxious, constantly pacing the floor and looking out the front window.

Emily went out of her way to make Jenn feel at home again. She cooked her favorite foods. They sat and watched movies together - just like old times. Emily thought that Jenn was beginning to relax and would soon open up. Still she refused to answer Emily's questions about where she had been, and whom she had been with. She wouldn't change her mind about going to the police.

"Jenn, I have an idea. When I get home from work tomorrow, how about we go to that little Italian place on Fourth Street for supper? We could both use an evening out."

"Sure mom. Anything you want."

CHAPTER TEN

The next evening, when Emily got home from work, her daughter was gone again. After that she never knew from one day to the next when Jenn was going to show up. Sometimes days passed, other times she would be home for a day or two, contrite, apologizing, and begging for forgiveness. Some days she was her old Jenn, bright, happy and full of plans for the future. Other times, she came home too sick to care. Those were the times Emily took a day off from work to hold her head while she vomited, and bathed her like a small child because she was filthy. Her first priority became trying to look after the welfare of her daughter. Each time Jenn came home Emily would sigh with relief. Her biggest fear was that one day she wouldn't.

There were times she also questioned the fact that if she had paid more attention to Ben or tried to understand him better, would their marriage have lasted, and could the accident have been prevented? She would never know for sure, but she was bound and determined not to do the same to her daughter. Whatever Jenn needed, or asked, for she got.

Elsie Jones, the office manager, was like a mother hen looking after and caring for everyone in the office. One day she questioned Emily about the amount of time she was taking off.

Emily was exhausted. Jenn had come home in the middle of the night, sicker than usual. At one point, she had debated about calling for an ambulance.

"Emily," Elsie said, "You look tired today. Is everything all right? Are you sick?"

"No, I'm fine, family problems."

"Your daughter?"

"Yes."

"Look let's get out of here for a while. Come have lunch with me. I forgot to make mine this morning."

Emily agreed to go with her, but she wasn't sure why. She wasn't hungry and Elsie was one of her least favorite people.

"Maybe a change of scenery and some food will do me good," she replied. "I was in such a hurry this morning that I left mine on the cupboard."

At noon they left their office, and walked around the corner to a small coffee shop. They had to wait for a table, and once they were comfortably seated Elsie said to Emily "I know this is none of my business Emily, but it is no secret around the office that your daughter has a severe drug problem. Is there anything I can do to help? My dear departed husband, God bless him, was an alcoholic, so I have an idea what you are going through."

Emily said nothing, moving her fork back and forth on her plate. She couldn't force herself to eat the spinach and strawberry salad she had ordered. After what seemed like a long time, she looked up and said, "I don't know what to do any more. Take last night. I was sound asleep when I heard the front door open and then somebody going up the stairs."

"Is that you Jenn?" I called out. When there was no answer, I got up and stood in the entrance of my bedroom door. She was crawling up the stairs - on all fours like she used to do when she was a baby.

She answered me saying, "I am fine mom honestly. Go back to sleep."

I flipped on a light, and her face and hands were covered with blood. I felt sick to my stomach. She was a mess, the worst I have ever seen her."

"What did you do?"

"I did what every mother would do. I cleaned her up, put her to bed, and then sat beside her all night to make sure she was still breathing."

"Did she tell you what happened?"

"No, she refused."

"Did you call the police?"

"No!'

"Why not?"

"I don't know, I don't think she would have wanted me to do that."

Elsie sat there quietly, and then asked," If this child were a stranger, and showed up at your front door in that condition what would you have done?"

"I would have called for an ambulance, and then called the police."

"Now I am going to ask you a hard question. If you would do

that for a stranger why wouldn't you do the same for your daughter? Why didn't you get her the help she needed?"

Emily looked at her and replied slowly, "I thought I was helping by doing what I could for her."

"I know that is what you thought, and as a mother you are absolutely right. You made yourself feel better because you were looking after her, but the more you do for her, the more she will expect. Your daughter is taking over your life and that's not right. You are entitled to have a life of your own without her being at the center. Somehow, and in some way, you have to stop letting her control your every thought and action. You have to take your life back. At some time we all reach a point where we have to say "enough is enough. I have done everything I can for you; the time has come for you to help yourself."

"How am I supposed to do that? She is my only daughter, she just turned sixteen. I can't turn my back on her," Emily replied angrily. Inside she was seething. *Just who the hell does she think she is anyway? I didn't ask for her advice and I am sure as hell not going to sit here and listen to anymore.*

She made a motion as if to stand up and leave but Elsie put her hand on her arm as if to stop her.

"I know you are thinking that I am interfering, but hear me out. I loved my husband even though he was a terrible drunk, but I deserved and made a life of my own. Think about what I have told you today. I work with a group of adults who are going through the same thing you are. We teach the parents that they need to look after themselves first, before they can help their kids. If you would like to come with me to a meeting, or decide you want more information, let me know."

They finished their lunch in silence. Emily was deep in thought. A lot of what Elsie said made sense, but she couldn't see how this applied to her. As they stood up to leave, Emily gave Elsie a big hug. "Thank you. Up until today I thought I was the only one facing this kind of a problem."

Elsie hugged her back. "Unfortunately Emily," she said, "You are one of too many. I am here to talk if you need someone."

When she got home from work that day she was excited. She had been looking forward to taking her daughter out for supper like they used to do. When she walked into the house it seemed very quiet. "Jenn," she called out, "I'm home."

There was no answer. The first thing she noticed when she walked into the living room was that her big screen television was gone. A further search showed Jenn was gone too.

CHAPTER ELEVEN

Several months passed and there was no word from her daughter. Emily felt like she was going through the motions of living; that everything she said and did seemed to be of no consequence. Several times she thought of calling the police but decided not to. Jenn would never forgive her if she did.

At least once every day she called Jenn's cell phone to hear her voice. Night after night, she drove around the town looking for her. Several times she thought she saw her, and her heart would skip a beat, but when the person turned around, it wasn't Jenn. She made posters and hung them on street corners. When she was doing this, she approached each person in the vicinity, showed them the picture, and asked if they had seen her daughter. Few people paid much attention to her. The poster gave her cell phone number, but there were no calls. Some nights she lay on Jenn's bed so she could feel close to her.

Then, in the middle of the night she was awakened by the sound of her cell phone ringing and vibrating on the bed side table. It stopped before she was able to answer it. She waited desperately in the dark to see if it would ring again. *Was it a wrong number? Was it Jenn trying to get hold of her?*

After what felt like forever, her phone rang again. This time she answered on the second ring.

"Hello. Who is this? Do you know have any idea what time it

is?"

"Mom, I need your help. Please come and get me, I don't want to be here."

Instantly she was awake. "Where are you Jennifer? What is going on? Are you okay?" She could hear her sobbing hysterically in the background. *Not again. Had those people caught her again?*

"Jenn calm down. Let me talk to someone who can tell me what is going on."

Soon the husky voice of Don Beatty came on the phone. She recognized it right away. "Mrs. Stuart, this is Don Beatty at the police station. We have your daughter here. I am sorry to inform you that she has been arrested for solicitation."

"What?"

"Because she is a minor, we allowed her to contact you. We will be keeping her overnight in a juvenile facility until her hearing tomorrow."

"I don't understand. What are you trying to tell me?"

"Mrs. Stuart, your daughter was arrested for solicitation which means she was offering sex to an undercover policeman. She is a mess, and strung out on drugs. When we asked her why she was doing this she told us this is how she pays for her drugs. Believe it or not this is the best place for her tonight. Then tomorrow, I suggest we try and find a place to put her into rehab. If you just take her home she will be gone again first chance she gets, and eventually we will end up picking up her body somewhere. There is nothing you can do tonight. Write down this phone number and call me in the morning. I will see what options are available, seeing this is her first offense."

"Is she that bad?'

"Yes, I am afraid she is. Call me in the morning if you are interested in getting her some help. In the meantime, I am going to see if there are any short term beds open that we can place her in."

Emily hung up the phone and cried until she fell asleep. She didn't know what to do any more, and there was no one to turn to for advice. She had tried every way she could think of to reach out to Jenn, but nothing worked.

When she asked for money Emily gave it to her. Jenn always had a story, like the time she was going to get her own apartment and needed money for the damage deposit. Sometimes it was because she owed money to someone and had to pay it back or else. The more Emily gave her, the more she demanded. Several times she had tried to firmly say no and stick to her decision, but eventually Jenn's begging and crying eventually wore her down. Each time Jenn left, she came home in worse shape than before. Every time Emily bailed her out, she hoped that this would be the last time, but there always seemed to be another. No matter what she did or how much money she gave, it was never enough.

This would be the third time she picked Jenn up at the police station and paid her fine. Jenn always promised never to do it again, but each time she was gone by the time Emily got home from work. *How did our lives ever come to this* she wondered?

She also wondered if the police charge was true. What could she have done differently to prevent this from happening? She was at a loss to figure it out. The thought of her daughter selling herself for drugs to any stranger on the street was more than she could bear. An ugly picture of men lining up to violate her daughter arose in her mind, but she tried desperately to shut that image out. *There was no way my daughter would stoop so low to do that so she could get her next fix. From now on Jenn will get whatever she asks for, anything, to stop her from prostituting herself for money to pay for drugs.*

It broke her heart to see the bruises on her daughter's body, and the ugly needle marks on her arms. Each time she took her in and tried to look after her, she looked thinner and more fragile.

May be a stint in rehab is the answer for both of us. In the last moment, before she fell into an exhausted sleep, she realized that she had run out of options. This was something she would have to do whether she wanted to or not.

CHAPTER TWELVE

She waited until nine-thirty before calling Don Beatty at the number he had given her the previous evening.

"Good morning Mrs. Stuart. I am pleased to hear from you. I was wondering if you would call me this morning. I am fully aware of how difficult this must be for you. I have been on the phone and found an emergency placement for your daughter at Amber House. They will hold a place for her until six o'clock this evening."

"What made you think that I wouldn't call?" Emily said sarcastically.

"No reason. It's that some parents prefer for me not to get involved. They want to try and do it themselves, or they have given up on their child and don't care anymore."

"You tell me if this is the right thing to do? I have been up all night trying to make a decision. Should I do this or should I bring her home, take some time off work, and look after her there".

"Have your tried this before?"

"Yes."

"How did that go for you?"

"She sneaked out in the middle of the night at the first opportunity she had. She used to come around when she needed money, but until last night I haven't seen or heard from her for several months. It's actually a relief to know where she is for once."

"Mrs. Stuart, do you love your daughter?"

Incensed at the question Emily replied "of course I do. If I didn't, I would have given up on her a long time ago. She is all I have."

"If you love her as much as you say you do, then do this for her. It's your choice. If you decide to make use of this perfect opportunity, meet me here at my office around eleven o'clock. Pack what clothes you have that are hers and anything else she might need, and bring them with you."

Don Beatty was tired. Yesterday had been a long day, and this was starting out to be another one. He had been called in when Jennifer was brought to the precinct station. He had been tempted to ask them to turn the case over to someone else, but, when he recognized the name of the daughter whose mother he had previously spoken with he felt it was his job was to follow her through the system, making sure no one took unfair advantage of her rights. Having already talked to the juvenile's mother once, he thought would make it a little easier to break the bad news. *Don, old boy*, he muttered to himself *remember, you can't save them all.*

Although he exercised on a regular basis at the gym, he was beginning to develop a paunch which was probably from sitting behind a desk all the time, and living on takeout food. He had also noticed that his hair was beginning to turn gray and getting thin on top. At five feet eleven inches he was of normal height, yet carried himself with the confidence of a man twice his size.

After his divorce, he noticed that the lines seemed to be etched deeper into his face

The last he heard from his ex-wife, Ann, was that she was moving to England to work. He was happy for her – she was doing exactly what she wanted. There was no room in a marriage for an ambitious wife who wanted to travel, and a cop who was dedicated to helping young girls living on the street. In the end, it had been an amicable divorce: both going their own separate ways and carrying no hard feelings between them. Thankfully there were no kids involved. His wife had been adamant about that. She didn't want to be tied down. Still, there were times he missed her and today was one of those days.

He took off his jacket and tie, loosened the top button of his shirt, and lay down on the old scarred, black, leather couch in his office. With any luck he would have time for a short nap before Mrs. Stuart arrived. He hoped that when push came to shove, Mrs. Stuart would be brave enough to do the right thing for her daughter.

Emily sat staring at the wall. *I wish I had stricter with Jenn. I should have been more forceful when all of this first started. At the time, getting over Ben and learning my new job seemed more important. I should have tried better to understand what Jenn was telling me. Maybe if I had insisted upon Jenn going to the school counsellor this could have been avoided*

Perhaps if I had learned to stand up to Ben our marriage would have been different, but that was something I will never know now. All through the years of our marriage Ben told me I was good for nothing. As far back as I can remember Ben always drank a little too much, but after Jenn was born he had gotten worse. It was almost as if he was jealous of the time and attention I lavished on my little girl.

She realized there wasn't much she could do about Ben now. She couldn't help him any longer. He had seen to that, but be damned. if she was going to lose her daughter too. *From now on I will do whatever I have to do to save Jenn.*

At exactly eleven she was at the police station waiting to be ushered into Don Beatty's office. Beside her was a small black and red flowered overnight bag containing the few articles of clothing Jenn had left at the house. On her way Emily had stopped at the drugstore and bought shampoo, tooth paste, a tooth brush, and, on impulse, the latest book by Jenn's favorite author. Also, tucked in one corner of the bag was a letter telling her how much she was loved and encouraging her to use this time to turn her life around.

"Mrs. Stuart?" Don Beatty asked as he approached the woman sitting outside his office. He was struck by how broken and distraught she appeared. "Come in to my office."

Emily sat down on a very old, scratched, wooden office chair. The office was small; a desk was covered with files, a computer monitor, and behind the desk a worn out, faded, gray swivel chair. A dilapidated black leather sofa occupied a side wall. The small dirty window provided little light, and the waste paper basket was overflowing onto the floor.

"I don't spend much time in here," he said apologetically, sweeping his arm around the room. "Guess it is kind of a mess. Mrs. Stuart…?"

"Call me Emily."

"Okay Emily, before I go into court, tell me more about your daughter. You told me about her dad being in jail the first time you called. How did she react to that?"

"Jen has always been a treasure, the perfect child. She was a cheer leader, vice-president of the student union and had lots of friend. She always seemed to be helping somebody. After Ben's accident, and he was convicted and sent to prison her friends turned away from her. She was bullied at school, her grades fell, and her best friends stopped coming over. There were people who boycotted the insurance company I worked for because I was there. Both of us had no choice but to try and make the best of a bad situation. Finally I divorced Ben, sold the house and got a transfer here. I was hoping we could start over again, just the two of us."

"Did Jennifer want to move?"

"No and neither did I, but it felt like we had no other choice."

"Go on."

'Everything seemed to start out well enough. At first I thought she was adjusting well, and then she began to change. We argued all the time, she was moody, defiant, and I found out she was skipping school.

She started drinking and partying with her new friends, and began staying out all night. I never knew where she was. I even found marijuana in her jeans pocket. One night we argued, and I slapped her. I didn't mean to, it just happened. I have never done that before. I tried to apologize, but she wouldn't listen to me. The next morning she was gone. She had taken two hundred dollars and my credit cards from my purse, and ran away.

When she came home she was a mess. She told me some kids from school took her to a cabin by a lake. The boys held her there for days, coercing her into doing drugs, and forcing her to have sex with them."

"Did you believe her?"

"Yes, why wouldn't I? Jenn doesn't make a habit of lying to me," Emily answered defensively.

"What did you do then? Did you call the police?

"No, she wouldn't let me. She said that she didn't want to get them involved. I took her in; she stayed home for three days, and then was gone again. Another time, after one of our arguments, I came home from work to find my big screen television missing."

"Can you tell me any more about what happened at the lake? Who took her there? Where was the cabin? Who was there with her?"

"No, you will have to ask her about that. She wouldn't tell me who was involved."

"Do you still believe her?"

"I want to, but I am having a hard time believing she would willingly put herself in that kind of a situation. I have always told her that if she needed a ride home, all she had to do was call, and I would have come and got her, no questions asked"

"Then what," he gently prompted. He knew the rest of the story. In one form or another he had heard it a dozen times. There would be one of two endings to this story. Either the kid stopped doing drugs and turned their life around, or turned their back on life, and became a slave to the drugs. For Emily Stuart's sake he hoped this was one of those stories that would have a happy ending.

"Emily, I am going to fill you in on what is going to happen today. Later this morning Jenn will come up before Judge Riley in juvenile court. I will be with her. She will most likely be fined on the solicitation charge, and as a condition of her release will have to go to a rehab facility. I will bring her outside to you and together we will take her to Amber House. Don't come into the courtroom. Once she is in the car, ignore her pleading and promises. Do your best not to show any emotions. Try to be matter of fact – this is just the way things are going to be for now. She knows that if she carries on long and loud enough you will give in."

"I don't know if I can do that."

"Emily do you love your daughter?"

"Yes."

"Then you have to."

CHAPTER THIRTEEN

At one o'clock that afternoon, Jennifer was brought into court to face Judge Riley. At one-thirty she walked out the front door of the court house with Don Beatty.

"Your mom is waiting in her car over there Jenn," he said, taking her elbow and guiding her toward the car.

"What's she doing here?"

"Waiting for you."

She smirked as she got into the front seat beside her mother. "Mom, I'm sorry, the other kids dared me. I wouldn't have gone through with it. Take me home. That place stunk, and I want to go home and have a shower."

Then Don Beatty climbed into the back seat.

"What's he doing here?"

Emily didn't answer her. She knew if she said anything, she would be in tears. She thought that seeing Ben sentenced, and sent to jail was the worst thing in her life, but that was nothing compared to this.

Don said, "let's go."

Cautiously she pulled out onto the street. The blood hammering in her ears and she felt nauseous. All was quiet in the car; a country and western radio station played in the back ground until she turned north and began driving out of town.

"Mom, this isn't the way home. Where are we going?"

Then Don Beatty spoke for the first time. "You're not going home Jennifer. Your mom and I are taking you to a rehab center known as Amber House. You will be staying there for the next sixty days. The court mandated this as part of your release today."

"Amber House – rehab, get serious. That place is for druggies and I'm not one of those. There is nothing wrong with me. Mom, tell him it was just a prank."

Emily gripped the steering wheel so hard her hands were white and aching. She could hear Ben saying, "the accident was not my fault," in the same whiney tone. Couldn't Jenn realize that she didn't want to do this? Sometimes love means you have to hurt the ones you love the most by going against their wishes, and doing what you think is right.

"Mom, stop this car," Jenn screamed. "You can't make me. Please don't do this to me. I will stop I promise. Please mom?"

Then she turned on Don Beatty. "This is your idea isn't it? If you hadn't put this in her head my mom wouldn't have enough guts to do this to me. Mom, I demand you stop this car right now or I will jump out. I am not going and that is that."

The drive seemed to take forever. Jenn alternately begged and cursed at her and Don Beatty. Emily stared straight ahead. Jenn's pleas were like a knife driving into her heart. Finally she drove through the black, wrought, iron gates into the yard of Amber house, and stopped in front of a door that said Admitting. As soon as she stopped Emily got out of the car and stood beside it shaking.

I want this to be over. If she doesn't walk through that door soon I am going to change my mind. We have come too far to have that happen.

Emily was surprised. Amber House was nothing like she expected. In her mind she had imagined an old Victorian brick house, like the ones you see in the movies. Instead, this building was modern, with lots of windows. It sprawled in front of her, looking more like a huge two story apartment complex. There were brightly, colored, flower beds and perfectly manicured lawns. Paths meandered in the grass leading to huge trees with wrought iron benches beneath them. In the center of the yard was a huge fountain, reminiscent of the ones she had seen in a book about Rome. The air was calm, peaceful and tranquil. Taking a deep breath, she forced herself to calm down. She knew she was doing the right thing for her daughter.

Don Beatty got out quickly and held the door open for Jenn. Seizing her by the elbow in a forceful grip he said, "Young lady, you are coming with me."

Jenn tried to pull away, but he tightened the hold on her arm. "You can't make me," she hissed at him. The look in her eyes defied him to continue.

"Look young lady. It's either this or a jail cell for the next sixty days. Your choice."

Emily opened the back door, and pulled out the bag she had packed for her daughter. Don Beatty took it in his other hand. When the two of them began walking up the sidewalk Emily ran to her daughter's side. "Jenn, I love you. I am doing this for your own good."

Jenn began screaming and cursing at her. Don Beatty hurried her along the sidewalk. The last words Emily heard her daughter say, as they went through the door, were, "I hate you, and you are a real bitch." I don't blame daddy for acting the way he did. You had it coming."

Don Beatty came out about an hour later. He found Emily sitting on a bench, under a huge maple tree in the front lawn. She was staring straight ahead; her face tear stained. He walked over, tapped her on the shoulder and said, "Let's go. She will be fine. She is going through the first stages of drug withdrawal. They are used to this kind of behavior, and will keep a close eye on her. Give me your keys, I'll drive."

Respectfully Emily handed him the keys and climbed into the passenger seat of her car. As they left the hospital grounds he asked, "When was the last time you ate?"

"I think it was yesterday. I'm not sure," Emily replied.

"I know a nice quiet little place, just down the road. How about if we stop there and get a bite to eat? The food is good, not too expensive and there is a nice quiet atmosphere." Then he added, "Emily, this is the right thing to do. Jennifer says she hates you right now, but hopefully one day she will thank you. In the meantime, you have to look after yourself."

At the diner they each ordered a burger, fries and a coffee. Two hours later they were still sitting there talking. She told him about Ben and their life together. For some unknown reason, he told her about his divorce. That was the first time he ever talked to another person about it.

During the time they sat there Emily started to relax - her

mood brightened. For a few days she would have something else to think about other than where Jenny was, who she was with, and what she was doing. Better yet, she knew Jenny was safe. For the first time in a long time she was hopeful. Besides she was enjoying sitting here with him.

After dropping Don off at his office she went home and felt a little more relaxed. That night she fell into a deep peaceful sleep as soon as she lay down.

As he watched her drive away Don told himself, *don't let her get to you big guy. The last thing you need in your life right now is another woman with a big problem.* But he knew it was already too late.

CHAPTER FOURTEEN

Don Beatty, for reasons best known to him, took an active interest in Jennifer Stuart's case. He usually tried not to get involved in the particulars of any case, learning long ago that once the kid was through the system and out the door, it was best to have no further dealings with them, unless they showed up again, or they were in the adult system.

Every day, for the first week he checked on Jinn's progress. The first few days she was sick, angry and resentful. Then, as the drugs cleared her system, she began to fully understand where she was, and why she was there. Every other day Don phoned Emily to give her a report on her daughter's progress. Emily was grateful for his calls.

On the tenth day he phoned Emily and asked, "What are you doing tomorrow?"

"I actually have the day off," she replied. "We alternate working four days a week at the office and tomorrow is my day to stay home. I am planning to be a lady of leisure for the day. Why do you ask?"

"I just finished speaking with the Director of Amber House. I was checking on your daughter's progress, and he suggested that now would be a good time to come and visit her. It so happens that I am off duty tomorrow, so if you are interested in going, I could drive you there?"

"Why Mr. Beatty, is this an official police request, or do I have a choice?" she teased.

"No, I just figured you might like to have someone with you. Since I have no plans for the day, I thought I would volunteer. That is, of course, if you want me to go with you."

"I would enjoy that very much sir."

"Good, I will pick you up around ten, your turn to buy lunch," he added.

When he picked her up the next morning, he was taken back. The last time he had seen her, she looked like hell. Her eyes were red and swollen from crying, her face was strained, and she appeared to be as fragile as a china doll.

This time she looked rested. Gone were the dark circles under eyes, and the strain from her face. She appeared relaxed and happy.

His heart skipped a beat. Up until now he hadn't realized how much he was looking forward to being with her today. He shook off the feeling. The last thing he needed was the complications of having a woman in his life. He was happy being alone, with only himself to look after. Besides, his erratic hours had been one of the reasons his marriage had failed. Most women couldn't handle being alone so much.

The drive to Amber House didn't take very long. They chatted about the unimportant things – the weather, how busy she was at the office, and so on. He regaled her with stories of when he was a rookie, and the funny cases he had attended.

He pulled up to the front door and said, "I'll let you out here.

I have a couple of errands to run, and then I will be back to get you, say in about two hours?"

"Take your time. If you aren't here when I'm finished, I'll be over by the fountain. I find the sound of water very soothing."

Emily was tense and worried about Jenn's reaction when she saw her. *Was this going to be another ugly scene or would they actually be comfortable being together?*

Taking a deep breath, and straightening her shoulders, she opened the front door and walked in. Looking around she noticed a sign that read Reception off to one side, she walked briskly over to the desk.

"Hello," she said. "My name is Emily Stuart. I am here to see my daughter Jennifer Stuart."

"She is excited and waiting for you in the study, third door on your left. We ask parents on their first visit to limit their time to one hour. This first meeting is equally difficult for you, as well as the patient. If you have time after your visit Director Jones would like to meet with you

"Yes, I have time."

"Good, stop here on your way out, and I will take you to his office."

Emily looked around. This was a beautiful place, more like a home than an institution. Walking down the hallway, and peering through the various open doors, she glimpsed a man-made lake behind the building. She was surprised, because it wasn't visible from the front. When she arrived at the door marked Study she saw Jenn sitting in an armchair toying with an open magazine.

"Jenn," she called out softly.

Jenn heard her, and squealing with delight, ran to her mother, threw her arms around her neck, and buried her head in her shoulder.

They stood there holding each other, both crying. Finally Emily detached herself, and led her daughter over to a coffee brown, leather couch which faced the tall windows. They sat there; neither of them speaking, hands entwined, both taking in the beauty in front of them, and feeling the peacefulness surrounding them.

Finally Emily asked," how are you Jenn? You look good." Then she added nervously, "this looks like a nice place to stay."

"Not bad for a jail," Emily snapped back, and then more gently said, "I am doing fine mom. I am looking forward to getting out of here and coming home."

"I am looking forward to that too."

Jenn told her about her room that she shared with another girl, their daily routines, the classes she was taking, and the single and group counselling sessions. Emily said little. She was content being with her daughter, even if it was only for an hour.

"Mom, I am sorry I did this to you". Jenn looked at her with tears in her eyes, "Will you ever be able to forgive me?"

"Jenn, you are my daughter. I will always love you, and so will your dad. Don't ever forget that."

"Mom, I lied to you."

Emily felt a brief twinge of anger. *Which time?* She said to herself, *there have been so many lies between us.*

"Mom, remember when I told you I was forced to stay out at the cabin by the lake, and couldn't escape to come home. Well that was all a lie. We were at the cabin, but we were partying. There were eight of us. The only reason I came home was because all the drugs and alcohol were gone, and nobody had any money left. That's where I met Skeeter. He looked after me."

Without thinking Emily retorted, "He looked after you so well that you had to sell your body to buy drugs?"

"Mom, please. I only do that when we run out of money. It doesn't mean anything. Skeeter doesn't want me to, but I do it to make him happy. He watches out for me and makes sure I am safe."

"Why Jenn? I don't understand why you did any of the things you have done. It makes no sense to me. I don't want to hear about Skeeter and what he does for you. That has nothing to do with this."

"I was confused." Then she started to cry again, "I am so sorry I did this to you. I know this isn't how you expected me to turn out. I know you wanted me to go to college and make something of myself. When I get home, I promise I will make this up to you. I promise to stay clean, find a job and pay back the money I stole."

Emily didn't know what to say or think. Her mind was reeling from what Jenn was telling her.

"Jenn I have to think about it. If you do move home, things would have to be different, you know that? I will insist on you going back to school, and continue with the counselling you are doing here."

Jenn nodded her head, "I know, I promise mom. I will really try. I will make you proud of me yet."

Emily looked at her watch. "I was told I could only stay for an hour today. I will think about all of this. I have next Wednesday off and will come back then."

"Mom, I love you. Please forgive me?" Jenn begged.

"I love you too baby," Emily replied. This was true, but after all Jenn had told her, she felt as though she couldn't make any promises to her daughter. *I need time to think this whole situation over. What will be best for me, and what will be best for Jenn?*

"My hour is up. I have to go now, but I will be back. I promise." Emily hugged her daughter one more time and slowly walked back down the corridor. When she turned and looked back Jennifer was standing in the doorway, watching her leave. The look on her face nearly broke Emily's heart. She wanted to go back, grab her by the hand, and take her home. But like it or not, she had to leave her there, and Jenn had to stay. Emily waved at her and blew her a kiss. Jenn waved back.

She was in shock at the enormity of her daughter's lies. She blamed herself. If she had known then what she knew now, things would have been a whole lot different.

When she arrived back at the Reception desk she was escorted to a small office down another corridor.

"Mrs. Stuart to see you" the receptionist said to a youthful looking man in dark rimmed glasses and long scraggly hair. He was wearing blue jeans with a hole in the knee, a tee shirt and sandals.

"Mrs. Stuart. Come in. I am Paul Jones. I understand you work with my mother at the insurance agency. She speaks highly of you. Come in and sit down. Can I get you anything?"

"No, I am fine thank you."

He sat down behind his desk. Folding his hands together he placed them on the desk, and looked at her. Emily felt like his eyes were boring through her as she sat in the green vinyl chair directly across from him. For some reason she felt intimidated, and ready to defend herself and her daughter.

"You are probably wondering why I asked you to stop today?"

"I presume it's so you can tell me how Jenn is doing."

"Physically she is doing well. She is gaining her strength back, but mentally and emotionally this is going to take longer," he stated in a matter of fact tone of voice. He sounded like he has said these same words hundreds of times before.

"I don't know what you mean. I don't understand any of this."

"Jennifer sees herself as a victim in all that's happened to her. It's her father's fault she is doing drugs, because he got into that accident and is in jail. It's your fault because you made her move here, and that's why she got mixed up with that group of kids. They made her do drugs. At no point is she ready to admit she made a choice, nor is she ready to take responsibility for her actions."

"Why would she think that? We moved here so I could protect her from the teasing and bullying at school. Why blame me?" Emily retorted.

"This way she doesn't have to own up to her actions. Until she realizes for herself that her life can be different I don't foresee much success for her treatment here. That's not to say her ideas won't change with a few more weeks of therapy. That is a very distinct possibility. After she leaves here I suggest further intensive counselling for her. I can give you the names of some good people who work with these situations."

"I was hoping that after she left here she would be cured, that our days of fighting would be over."

"Mrs. Stuart, this is only the first step in a very long journey. I hope you seriously consider more intensive counselling. Another thing I suggest is that you begin saying no to her. She has you wrapped around her little finger, and if I am not mistaken, gets everything she asks for. It is more important now than ever that you set limits on how much you are willing to do for her. The limits need to be in place before you take her home so she understands that things really are going to be different."

Emily stared at him. She didn't know what to say. Nobody had ever spoken to her in this way about Jenn before. "I have already told her she would have to go back to school and have more counselling."

"That's a good start. Mrs. Stuart, but you will need to stick to your word and not back down. She is going to fight your authority any way she can. You will have to be tough. I don't know if you are aware that my mom works with a group of parents who have, or are facing the same problems as you. We offer a program through a group known as AHPCAD, Amber House Parents Council against Drugs. I know she will be more than willing to work with you."

Emily was angry. She stood up to leave, extending her hand politely to Mr. Jones. "Thank you," she said, "I have to think about all of this. All I know is that I want my daughter back and will do whatever it takes." Then she left.

Paul Jones shook his head. He sincerely hoped they got through this, but he had his doubts. Emily Stuart was in denial, and until she began to face the reality of the situation, nothing was going to change. Jennifer Stuart would be back.

Don Beatty was waiting outside for her by his car. The first thing he noticed was that the haunted look on her face had returned.

When she got into the car she looked at him and said vehemently, "I am really ticked off. Who is he to tell me what to do? I know what's best for my daughter. I don't need some stranger trying to tell me what is right or wrong." He let her ramble on and on. It would be good for her to get her anger out now.

Finally he interrupted her. "Do you want to stop for lunch Emily, your turn to buy today?"

He wasn't going to get caught up in her anger. He had seen this same attitude too many times, and he knew eventually she was going to need to face the truth. Today was not that day.

"Sure" she replied. "Sorry for going off like that. This isn't your problem."

Within minutes they were sitting in the diner in a quiet booth towards the back. "What did he say to you that has you so upset?" Don asked.

"I thought she would be cured, but he tells me she needs more counselling – that Jenn blames her dad and me for all of this. We weren't the ones that stuck a needle in her arm. Furthermore, he thinks I should join their support group and learn how to look after my daughter. I have been looking after her all of her life. Besides, I'm not going to sit around with a bunch of people feeling sorry because their kids are on drugs."

He let her spout off. When she calmed down he asked, "How is Jenn?"

"She looks good. I don't know what to think though. She confessed to me that her story about being held at the lake was a lie, and that she wanted to be there. She made it sound like going out on the street to have sex with strangers was not a big deal, that it is was the only way to get enough money to pay for her drugs. Then she tells me that she does this for some guy named Skeeter, and he looks after her. I sure as hell didn't teach her that behavior was okay. I came away with the impression that this Paul Jones guy doesn't hold out much hope for her."

Don felt sick. Jenn was in the clutches of a pimp, and he controlled everything she did. He had heard of this guy before. Plainly Emily had no idea what was really going on.

"Emily, I am in no position to tell you what to do, but maybe he does have a good point. He has worked with a lot of kids like Jenn. Did you even stop to think he might know what he is talking about?"

"Don't you start too," she replied.

Reaching over, he patted her hand and left his resting on top of hers. She smiled shyly at him, but didn't pull her hand away. "I told him I would have to think about all of this. I still have a few weeks before she is discharged.

CHAPTER FIFTEEN

On schedule, five weeks later, Emily drove out to Amber House and brought her daughter home. Jenn was excited, full of promises and ideas. Emily was content to have her daughter under her roof again.

All went well for the first week, and then Emily noticed that Jenn was becoming more withdrawn and spending more time alone in her room. The adjustment had been hard for both of them. Emily didn't trust Jenn; she could leave again at any time. For the first few days supper was ready when Emily got home from work, but after a while she noticed that Jenn had neither bathed nor dressed for days at a time. She wanted to say something, but she didn't. In her heart she knew Jenn was using again.

She was upset with her daughter, but, in reality, more upset with herself. She meant to be strong and enforce the rules they had agreed upon, but unconsciously they fell back into the old familiar pattern. All of her good intentions went out the window.

A month after Jenn returned, Emily came home from work to find her house in shambles. The place had been completely torn apart and Jenn was anxiously pacing the floor.

"Jenn, what in the hell happened here today?" she said angrily. "Look at this mess. Did you do this?"

"I need money."

"If you needed money, why didn't you ask?" Suddenly Emily realized her daughter was high. "Are you using again? You promised not to."

"Mom, please no lectures I really need some money. Skeeter was here. He needs the money and I told him I would get some. I owe him."

"Did he do this?"

"Please mom, he really needs it, and I have to pay him back."

"For what, turning you into a prostitute?" Emily was livid.

"Mom, you don't understand. It's not like that. He loves me."

"Well I am not giving you any. Now clean this place up, while I make supper. I will never give you money to support your habit, and I will not give you money to give to that Skeeter creep."

She was turning to go into the kitchen, when out of the corner of her eye, she saw Jenn grab her purse and move toward the door. "You leave that alone!" she yelled, making a grab for the strap.

Jenn drew back her fist, and punched her mother in the stomach. Emily fell to the floor and watched as her daughter rummaged through her wallet, taking all of the cash and her credit cards. Then, without looking back, she calmly walked out the door.

Emily lay on the floor for a long time clutching her abdomen and wondering what had just happened. *How was she able to start using drugs again? Who was giving them to her?*

For the first time she realized that Skeeter, whoever he was, had more influence over her daughter than she did. Jenn must have phoned, and told him she was home. Trashing Emily's house was his way of showing her who was in control.

She never felt so helpless in her life. Instinctively, she knew that if she didn't fight for her daughter, Jenn would be lost to her forever.

Desperately Emily tried to call Don Beatty to let him know of these new developments and get his advice, but his phone repeatedly went to voice mail. Each time, instead of leaving a message, she hung up.

CHAPTER SIXTEEN

.

Emily raged into the night. *What is wrong with that kid? Can't she see that she isn't only hurting herself but everyone around her? There are people who love and care about her. Can't she at least consider their feelings? The whole world doesn't revolve around Jennifer so why does she think it should?*

Like a caged animal Emily paced back and forth in her living-room slowly beginning to understand what Don was trying to tell her. The way she had been trying to deal with Jenn's problems was getting her no place. Every time she overlooked the fact that money was missing from her purse, or that something else had disappeared from the house, she wasn't helping either of them. If her daughter was ever going to get off drugs she had to stop blaming her mother and her father's accident, and understand that she was the only person responsible for the mess she was in. The question was - how was she going to do that?

Emily also realized that by covering up for her daughter, taking responsibility for her actions, and making excuses was empowering Jenn. She now understood she had done the same thing with Ben, and look how that ended. As long as Emily continued doing what she was doing, Jenn would keep doing what she was doing.

She loved her daughter more than anything else in the world. Jenn was all she lived for, but was she helping or hindering the situation they were in? Perhaps Don was right. To really show Jenn how much she loved her, Emily was going to have to stop what she was doing, put some rules and boundaries in place, and stop letting Jenn walk all over her.

She tried to reach Don at his office number at seven a.m. "I am ready to listen to you now" she said, when he answered. "I am willing to do whatever it takes to get my beautiful daughter back."

"Emily, I hope you realize that this is going to be the hardest thing you have ever done in your life, and harder on you than on her. Once you start, you can't change your mind."

"I know, but I don't know what else to do," she replied, her voice quivering. "If things don't change, the drugs are going to kill her." Then, in a much stronger more determined voice she asked, "what do I do first?"

"Call a locksmith and have him change the locks on your doors. Make sure all of your unused windows are locked, and have someone come in and change the outdoor lights on your house and garage to motion sensor lights."

"Am I doing the right thing Don? I feel like I am turning my back on her. What if this doesn't work? She will hate me forever."

"For now she will, but once we get her straight, clean and sober she will thank you for taking a stand. She'll get over it, you'll see, and one day, far into the future, she will thank you, but for now it is going to be a rough ride. Another suggestion I have is to talk to that lady you work with, you know the one who works with the Amber House program. She has the experience, knowledge and resources to help you through this." Then, in a softer more personal tone he said, "Emily, you can do this."

"I know, but I don't want to. It seems now I don't have a choice anymore."

"If you need me, you know that I am here for you."

"I know," she replied "thank you for being such a good friend."

After she hung up the phone, Emily curled up in her favorite, green, recliner chair and cried. She knew everything Don told her to do was right, but why did it feel so wrong?

Still she was not ready to give up on her daughter. Her mind was telling her to stop – to give up, enough was enough, but her heart was unwilling to accept the inevitable

For the next three weeks she kept to herself. She took time off from work, and avoided both Don's and Elsie's phone calls. She spent most of her time berating herself. *This is all my fault. Look what happened to Ben. If I had been a better wife, he wouldn't have had to drink so much. If I had been a better, more understanding mother, Jenn wouldn't be in this terrible situation.*

Late at night she would get into her car and drive up and down the streets, searching for her daughter. She didn't know for sure what she would do if, and when. she found her.

Then one night the inevitable happened. She saw Jenn getting out of a car, and take her place with the other girls on the sidewalk. She looked terrible, nothing but skin and bones. She was dressed in a tight, short, black, leather skirt, low cut top and very high heels - she looked like a child playing dress up.

She pulled over to the curb, parked her car, and joined the people milling around on the sidewalk. Cars cruised up and down the street, gawking at the girls standing there. She stayed close to the building because she didn't want Jenn to run away when she saw her.

When she was close, she grabbed Jenn by the arm and began screaming at her. "You are coming home with me. Get into my car right now. What on earth do you think you are doing?"

"Mom, go away. I don't need you coming here and telling me what to do." Jenn began backing down the street away from her mother. Emily hung onto her arm as tightly as she could and began pulling her down the street toward her car.

"Young lady, you are coming home with me and that is final."

"Mom, leave me alone. You don't understand. Go away before you get hurt."

Emily kept trying to drag Jenn down the street when suddenly a man's voice behind her sneered "take your hands off her."

A man, twice her daughter's age, appeared beside Jenn. He had long, greasy, dark hair pulled into a pony tail, and a blue shirt, open to the waist that shimmered in the street light. He wore a large diamond pendant around his neck and a diamond earring in his left ear.

"Take your hands off of her right now," he said menacingly, forcing his way between mother and daughter,

"Skeeter stop," Jenn cried out," it's my mom."

Emily stopped trying to drag her daughter, but didn't let go of her arm.

"And what may I ask do you think you are doing?" he snarled at her.

Taking a deep breath, and drawing herself to full height Emily replied, "I am taking my daughter home, and don't you try to stop me."

"Jenn," he purred "is that what you want baby? Do you want to go home with her, and go through hell again or stay with me, and let me look after you?"

Jenn started to cry and replied, "Go home mom. I'll phone you later."

"No, I am not leaving until you come with me."

"Please Skeeter, let me talk to her? Mom, let's go over here and talk this over."

"I've had enough of your interference," he said to Emily putting his face right up to her. "She stays with me." Then he turned to Jenn and said, "you know what the consequences are if you leave with her. Eventually you will be back. I have had enough of this crap, and when you do, I am going to talk to Pete about putting you on his corner permanently. If you think this is bad you won't think so after spending a little time with him. After a couple of days, you will be begging me to take you back."

Jenn's face turned pale. She looked at her mother sadly and said, "Go home mom. I have to stay with Skeeter. He looks after me. Please try to understand that."

"Good choice," he said, reaching over and lifting Emily's hand off her daughter's arm. "Stay away from her. Do you understand me?"

"Are you threatening me? I will go to the police."

"Take it any way you want bitch, but if you want to see your daughter again, you will go home and forget about this." Then he grabbed Jenn's arm and dragged her away. She could hear him yelling at her, but her replies were indistinguishable

Emily stood there until they disappeared down the alley, and then slowly walked back to her car. Once she thought she could hear her daughter screaming, but didn't dare go back. She felt as if part of her was ripped away. Jen had chosen Skeeter over her, and she had never felt so helpless in her life.

CHAPTER SEVENTEEN

After another long night and as soon as she knew the office was open the next morning, she phoned Elsie. "Is it possible for me to have today off? I've been up all night."

"Why, what's going on? Is everything all right? Are you sick?'

"No, It's Jenn." She broke down; trying to explain between sobs what had taken place. She was so distraught that she didn't know if she was making any sense. Finally she added, "Elsie, remember that day we had lunch you offered to help me?"

"Do you mean about attending the meetings?"

"Yes. Tell me what I need to do. I am desperate," Emily replied.

"Look Emily, take the rest of the week. Fortunately there is meeting this evening. I can stop by after work and pick you up?"

"I would like that. What time will you be here?"

'If all goes well, I should be there just after five. We'll grab a quick bite to eat and then go from there."

Emily gave Elsie her address, and then went to have a shower, and get dressed. Her heart was heavy, and her actions slow. For the very first time, she fully comprehended the fact that her daughter was gone, and was replaced by a stranger whose sole purpose was to have enough money to pay for her next fix.

Emily knew she was on the edge – in fact she wondered if she wasn't in the midst of having a nervous breakdown. First Ben, now this, she didn't know how much more she could take.

Before the day was over, and after talking with Don, she reported the theft of her cash and credit cards to the police. That way the police would have the information on record. As a precautionary measure Don had the police watching out for Jenn.

He was going to try to find her and get her into protective custody before Skeeter moved her. He knew he had to work fast. When there was trouble, Skeeter moved his girls to another town, and sometimes they never came back.

When she explained to the locksmith she had been robbed he immediately came over and changed the locks. He also recommended installing a security system and would return the next morning to install it in for her. She also made arrangements for an electrician to install motion sensor lights in the back yard.

By the time five o'clock rolled around she was exhausted. *Maybe I should call Elsie back and tell her I have changed my mind,* but she didn't, Instead she decided to take Elsie's offer to help and not hurt her feelings. *I will go this one time, and then find an excuse not to go to any more. After all, I was the one who phoned her.*

Emily was elated when Elsie called to say she was going to be late. This way they didn't have time to go for supper. As it was, she was extremely anxious. As soon as Elsie drove up, she ran out to the car, before she changed her mind. Elsie drove to St. Pauls' church located on the other side of town. Leading her down a flight of stairs, they entered a small conference room in the basement.

The room was small and cozy. A fire was flickering in the gas fireplace, and along one wall was a table with tea, coffee, cookies and sandwiches. The room was set up with ten round tables with chairs for six people. Set at each place was a series of pamphlets.

What surprised Emily the most was that there were at least twenty people already in the room, and several more came in behind them. All this time she thought she was the only person facing this problem and it made her feel better. There was a mix of people from grandparents to teenagers, many alone like her.

"Christy, I want you to meet Emily. This is her first meeting with us." Elsie said, introducing her to a woman standing at the front of the room.

"Emily, this is Christy McPherson, our group leader. Christy is responsible for the development of the outreach program with Amber House, and is the reason we are all here tonight."

A few minutes later, after each person had settled at a table, Christy moved to the front and began to speak, "I want to welcome all of our newcomers tonight. We are pleased that you have joined us. Please stand up, introduce yourself by your first name."

Emily was surprised to see there were three other new people besides her. Emboldened by the fact when her turn came she stood up and announced, "My name is Emily. My seventeen year old daughter is a drug addict and a prostitute. I want to help her."

Everybody clapped. Some murmured, "Welcome Emily."

Then Christy began to speak. "Many of you know my story, but for the sake of our new comers, I am going to tell it again."

Somebody in the back groaned, "Not again." Everyone giggled. The tension in the room was broken.

"Five years ago I was on the fast track to success with an advertising agency in the city. The job was thrilling, and I was having the time of my life. To me, life was one big party. I began drinking heavily on weekends, and then during the week, alone in my apartment. Most nights I didn't stay home, and usually went to a club located down the street. More often than not, I would wake up in the morning with a terrible hangover and a strange man in my bed not knowing what happened. The more I did this, the more disgusted I became with myself.

After one particularly bad night a co-worker offered me an upper to help me get through the day. At night it was booze, in the day time uppers to keep functioning. After about nine months of this, I was fired. I stayed and drank in my apartment until I was evicted for not paying my rent and ended up living on the streets. Somehow I managed to survive.

A few months later, I was arrested for being drunk and disorderly. I hit the cop with my purse and got three months for assault. While I was in jail I got sober, and have been ever since. I moved here from the city, got a student loan, and went back to school at night. In the day time I worked as a waitress in a coffee shop. I decided I wanted to help other women who are caught up in the same trap I fell into.

Then I heard about Amber House. I joined a volunteer program and chose to work here. My parents had disowned me when they saw what I was becoming. They refused to help me in any way. They insisted on telling me that I was the only one who could help me. At the time I was extremely angry with them, but as usual they were right. I think that is something we have all had to learn in one way or another.

Each person here this evening is reaching out for help. Some are new, just beginning their journey to recovery; others are here for the continued positive reinforcement that we offer. Whatever your reason, we are on this journey together.

I see some of you wondering what I mean by recovery. Most often people show up here when they are at an all-time low, and don't know what to do anymore. Recovery means getting your life back. You deserve to live a life of happiness, not despair and sorrow. Our addicted children or spouses, their neediness, and our desire to make it better have zapped all of the energy we have. The plain truth is we cannot help others unless we look after ourselves first. You are the only one who can do this for you."

The room broke out in a murmuring of consent. This wasn't what Emily expected. She thought she was going to be told easy ways to help her daughter.

After the hour long meeting, Emily and Elsie went to an all-night coffee shop and talked for hours.

"Emily," Elsie said, "we base our meetings and recovery on what we refer to as tough love. Have you ever heard of that?"

"No, what is it? What do you mean by that?" Emily asked.

"Tough love is basically loving a person so much that you take a stand and stop enabling their behavior," Elsie said. "You learn to say no. You stop making life easy for them by refusing to give into their demands. You tell them, "I love you so much I'm not going to enable you anymore. It's not helping you, nor is it healthy for either one of us."

If you're addicted child asks for money you refuse to give it to them. I will warn you, they can become very devious, coming up with excuses as to why you should, but you continue saying no. If they want to come home, you tell them 'not while you are addicted. You know I don't allow drugs in my place. When you are clean and sober we will discuss this again." You put limits on what you are willing to do for them, and then both of you live within these limits.

My husband tried hard to blame everything on me. His drinking was my fault. We would fight about his drinking, and I would take the kids and leave. He would quit, and I would go back. Each time it was the same; after a month or so we were back at each other again, each time worse than the last."

Elsie paused as a waitress refilled their coffee cups, and then she continued. "I heard about Christy's group, and after one particularly bad spell, I realized I had to do something or I would kill myself. I phoned Christy late one night. She didn't know who I was but she got out of bed and came and picked me up. She helped me realize that I needed to put my energy into controlling what I could, instead of wasting it on what was beyond my control. When I began attending the meetings on a regular basis, I learned, in a positive way, some coping skills, to stop blaming myself, and how to become a better parent."

"It wasn't easy," Elsie added, "but slowly I began to accept life as it is, not what I wanted it to be. Also, I learned that I wasn't alone. There were many others just like me feeling isolated and alone. Since then I have made it my mission in life to reach out, and help others feeling the same as I did."

We sat in this same coffee shop and talked all night." Elsie continued "Christy helped me realize that I was enabling him every step of the way. I had to give up owning the problem and find what would make me happy. Nothing I said, or did was going to make a difference until he faced up to the fact that he had a serious drinking problem."

"Did he quit?" asked Emily.

"Not until he was diagnosed with liver cancer. Then it was too late."

"What exactly are you trying to tell me."

"Emily, when you see your daughter, what do you see?"

"I don't understand."

"I'll rephrase my question. What were your plans for Jenn?"

"I see her as valedictorian for her class, going to college, getting married, giving me grandchildren. I wanted her to have everything I didn't have." Emily replied, her eyes filling with tears.

"Do you still have this picture in your mind?"

"I guess, well yes. That's why I don't understand any of this."

"Do you have any idea how Jenn sees her future?"

"I hope it is the same."

"She sees it as getting through to her next fix, having sex with as many men as it takes to earn the money she needs. She will do whatever has to be done so that Skeeter doesn't beat her again. As for tomorrow, all she sees is more of the same. Her whole life revolves around making sure she has enough money to buy her drugs. She knows that she has let you down, but is incapable of making the decision to make her life any better."

Emily was quiet. Inside she was screaming *I don't want to hear this. Stop!*

"What are you thinking?" Elsie asked gently. She could see how much Emily was hurting.

"I'm not sure, part of me doesn't want to believe you, the other part knows what you are saying is true. I am so afraid that one day the police are going to show up on my doorstep, and tell me she is dead."

"I can understand that, but you can't sit and worry."

"I know, but I can't help it. She is so thin and fragile that looking at her scares me. There is practically nothing left of her. When she is home she is twitchy, some part of her is always moving. I don't know what to do any more."

"There is nothing you can do. She will have to hit rock bottom, before trying to help herself. She tried when she was in Amber House, but the reason that failed was because she was forced to be there. It wasn't her choice. She wasn't ready to accept the help they were giving her.   Emily, you also have to realize this is not your fault. It would be different if you had handed her the drugs and told her take them, but you didn't. I don't know why your daughter started using drugs, but she did.

128

We don't know why people do a lot of the things they do. Now she is the only one who can make herself stop."

"What you are saying doesn't make me feel any better."

"It's not supposed to; it's to make you think," Elsie replied.

"How hard are you willing to fight for her? Up until now you have given into Jenn- given her whatever she wanted – feeling sorry for her – blaming yourself. If you truly love your daughter, you need to get your head in the real world, and see her for what she is."

"I see what she has become. If she hadn't got mixed up with that group at school, if Ben hadn't drank so much, if I had stayed home more …."

"Emily stop! Do you hear yourself? Those are Jenn's excuses for using drugs and you are buying into them. That's not what she needs right now."

"Do you have any better suggestions?" Emily replied sarcastically.

"I do. Like I told you, stop giving into her. No more money, no more letting her come home so she can steal from you. No more buying into her excuses. Take a stand for once in your life."

Emily was seething with anger. It was taking everything she had not to tell Elsie to shut up and mind her own business.

Then gently Elsie said, "Emily you have two choices. You can keep on doing what you are doing and nothing will change. But if you give Jenn an ultimatum, she will have something to look forward to, something that will give her hope."

"What kind of ultimatum?"

"You could tell Jenn, you love her and you want to help her, but until she is clean and sober there is little you can do. And then follow through. Learn to say no and stick to your principles."

The two of them sat in silence. Emily felt her anger drift away. She noticed a young boy, not more than sixteen, enter the coffee shop and sit in a back booth. The waitress brought him a cup of coffee. The next time she looked, she noticed he had fallen asleep, his head resting on an outstretched arm, and his coffee getting cold. She returned her attention to Elsie.

"Does this approach work?" Emily asked.

Elsie replied "Sometimes, but not all the time. There is a better chance of success using this approach than if you keep giving into her. Besides what more have you got to lose? You are already losing your daughter to drugs and the street. There are agencies and people available to help her but first it has to be her choice. In the meantime we are here for you."

Emily looked at her friend, tears brimming in her eyes, "There has to be another way. I don't think I can do that. I love her, she is my only child."

"Your daughter has made her choice. Until she hits bottom, and owns up to the fact she has a problem, she is not going to change. Nothing you say or do is going to make a difference. When you finally accept this, you can begin building a life that makes you happy. You don't disown her or give up on her, but you stop basing every move, and every decision you make around her. That is what I had to do. I never stopped loving my husband, but the children and I lived a life that he wasn't part of. It wasn't easier, but it was healthier. I stopped nagging him and fighting with him about his drinking, and he learned to set a few rules in place for himself. We were all with him when he died.

Emily, you have a daughter with a very serious drug addiction. You have done everything you can for her, but there is still one more thing you can do".

"What is that?" questioned Emily.

"Learn to say no, turn her away, Stop letting her control your life. If she comes to you and asks for money because she is hungry, take her and feed her. Don't give her money for groceries because she won't buy them. She will use it for something else. If she wants to come home, agree that she can as long as she is clean and doesn't bring any drugs into your house. You set the limits. Lock up your valuables; change the locks on the door, and from now on stop making it easy for her. If you want more years with her, you have to try. It is entirely up to you. This is a decision only you can make.

Your first step is acceptance - like it or not that's the way it is. Pray for courage and strength to do what is right, not easy or convenient. Accept help- you can't do it all yourself, and finally turn this over to God, and let him do what he has to do."

"Elsie, I 'm not a religious person. This prayer thing- I don't know anything about that."

"All you have to do is whisper and know a higher power is listening. This is out of your hands. You have done all you can for your daughter up until now, besides what can it hurt?"

"Nothing," Emily replied. "I can use all of the help I can get. Not to change the subject, but have you noticed that young boy, sleeping in the booth over there? I wonder why the waitress hasn't woken him up and made him leave."

Elsie turned and looked at him. "He probably feels safe here because he has no place to go. There are lots of kids out there living on the streets. As long as he is quiet and not bothering anyone the staff will leave him alone. It's a pretty rough world out there."

Elsie motioned to the waitress to come over. When she arrived, coffee pot in hand, Elsie handed her ten dollars and a business card. "When that young fellow wakes up, give him a decent breakfast and this card. He can find help there if he needs it."

CHAPTER EIGHTEEN

When Emily finally got home that evening she had a lot to think about. In a strange way, she felt a sense of relief because now she knew she was not alone. She was beginning to understand what happened to Jenn, and that it wasn't her fault. She was also grateful to Elsie for showing her that there were other people dealing with the same problems.

Elsie had given her the rest of the week off, and Emily developed a plan she wanted to follow up on. She wanted to see for herself what kind of environment her daughter was trapped in. Knowledge was power, and she was determined to find out all she could.

All the next day she tried to figure out what her next move should be. She was sure now that her daughter was lost to the streets and drugs, but she wasn't prepared to give up on her yet. Ben had made his choices, now Emily was making hers. The time had come for her to stop feeling responsible. All the time, money, and energy she had put in to helping both of them had only helped prolong the deception and the agony.

She arranged to meet Don for lunch to talk her idea over with him. "Don, I need to do this. I am going to the East end and find out for myself. I need to know what I am up against."

"Do you think that is a wise move? That part of town is not a safe place to wander around in. Besides, what do you expect to gain from going there?" he asked, trying to dissuade her.

"I 'm not sure, maybe I will catch a glimpse of Jenn, and see that she is at least alive – I am not even sure myself why, but it feels important. I feel like this is the right thing to do."

The next evening she put on a pair of sneakers, old jeans and a denim jacket. She wanted to try and blend into the street as best she could. She drove across town and parked in front of a shabby convenience store, so there would be lights around her car when she returned.

She had questioned her motives all day. Did she really want to know how her daughter was living, but the feeling was so strong she had to go.

Walking down the street, she could see this was a completely different world than what she was used to. The hotels were shabby and seedy. Some had signs in the front window "Available by the hour, day or week." Some of the doorways, recessed from the street, smelled of urine. In one she saw a young couple huddled under a sleeping bag, trying to get some sleep.

Cars were cruising up and down the street. One of them pulled alongside Emily. The passenger rolled down the window and an older man asked, "how much for both of us?"

With her heart in her throat she ignored them and kept on walking. She didn't know what she would do if someone tried to grab her. She noticed small groups of women standing on the street corners. Some were so young they looked like babies. Others were older and hard looking. On several other corners she noticed young men standing around as aimlessly as the women. As she watched, a car pulled up and a boy got in. She didn't need to guess what that was all about. There was no sign of Jenn.

Suddenly, she felt overcome with panic. Turning around in the middle of the sidewalk she started running back to her car. A hand reached out and grabbed her arm, and a hoarse voice said "where are you going pretty lady?" She yanked her arm away and ran as though a pack of banshees were chasing her. If anyone got in her way, she pushed them aside. All she wanted to do was get away from this place.

She located her car, and still in a panic raced home. Once in the house, she ran into the bathroom and was violently ill. All she could think about was her beautiful daughter who, for whatever reason, was living like those young men and women, and she had no idea what she could do. Trying to calm herself, she had a warm bath and put on her robe.

She was making herself a cup of tea when the front door bell rang. Peeking through the slightly open door she saw Don standing there.

'Hi," she said surprised, "what are you doing here?"

"I was driving past. I wanted to make sure you got home safely," he replied.

Opening the door she let him in, and then her brave facade crumpled as she was trying to tell him she was fine. He reached out for her and wrapped her in his arms, kissing her on the top of her head, as if he were comforting a child. He was murmuring in her hair, "thank God you are okay. I never should have allowed you to go there by yourself. I was worried that something terrible was going to happen to you."

She pulled her head away from his chest, and looked up at him helplessly. Her eyes reminded him of a wounded animal. Don could see that whatever had happened was more than she could bear.

Putting his hand under her chin, he lifted her face up toward him, kissing her first on her forehead, and then her lips. At first she resisted slightly, and then the passion between them flared. They began kissing, neither one of them wanting the other to stop.

He pulled away from her and softly asked "are you sure?"

"Yes," she replied.

He picked her up, carried her to her bedroom and laid her gently on the bed. She lifted her arms and pulled him to her. Their frantic joining fulfilled a primitive passionate need in both of them – the need to love and be loved in return.

For Emily, it had been a long time since someone had held her. She needed to feel safe, to feel loved, but most of all to feel like a woman again.

Afterward, laying side by side not looking at each other, Don said, "I have wanted to make love to you from the first time we had lunch, but I didn't come here with that in mind tonight. It was just that you looked so vulnerable, so broken that I needed to comfort you. Believe me, this was not my intention for coming here."

"I know" she replied, "Please don't apologize. I could have stopped you, but I needed someone to hold and love me, even if only for a short time."

He turned toward her, and placing his hand under her chin, kissed her gently. In response she turned onto her side and gathered him into her arms. This time their love making was more leisurely, each aware of the needs of the other, each giving all they had.

When she awoke the next morning he was gone. She felt a contentment in her body that she hadn't felt for a long time. Her mind was a blur of senses and feelings. That terrible environment Jenn was forced to work in, those men driving around, and the hand that grabbed at her. Intermingling with those was feeling Don's hands on her and in her, her tears after their mutual climax, and the peace she felt laying in his arms.

As long as she lay there, she could feel the glow of their love making and the tranquility enveloping her. Jenn was not part of this world. She wished Don was still next to her, so she could kiss him awake and make love to him again.

Reluctantly she forced herself out of bed. This was a new day, but as soon as she stood up, her fears and anxiety crashed into her; overwhelming her senses, tearing away that languid contented feeling she was experiencing only moments before.

Even though they had been together Emily forced herself to think of Don as more of a friend than a lover. She hesitated to admit to herself that she was in love with him.

The next time they met she forced herself to say, "I care deeply for you, but I can't get romantically or sexually involved right now. There is too much happening, and it's not fair to lead you on. Up until the other night the only man I have ever been with is Ben, and I'm not sure of my feelings right now. I feel vulnerable and confused. Can you understand what I am trying to say? Right now I need a good friend more than anything." She knew by the look on his face that her words were hurting him.

After a moment of silence he finally replied, "I understand. To tell you the truth I haven't even thought of another woman since Ann and I were divorced, but I want what is best for you." What he really wanted was to make love to her again and again, but she was so emotionally fragile that to push her now would be to lose her.

Grateful for his understanding, Emily hugged him tightly. "Thank you. Maybe after I get Jenn straightened out we will have time for each other. I hope so. You mean too much to me to ever lose you."

What she really wanted was for him to crush her in his arms and disagree with her. In the meantime she would hold onto the memory of the night they shared.

CHAPTER NINETEEN

Emily continued to attend the meetings with Elsie. Slowly she began to understand that she could learn to live for herself, and stop obsessing about her daughter. She began to feel stronger, and more in control of what was happening around her.

Several times her cell phone rang in the middle of the night, and each time it was Jenn begging for money. Each time, and as much as it hurt her, she forced herself to say no. She kept hoping that the next time would be easier, but it never was.

Emily and Don had developed a new kind of closeness. Not the lets jump in to bed kind, but the comfortable closeness of two people who love and care for each other. Their one night of love making formed a deep personal bond between them.

If the truth was known Emily was afraid. Although she and Ben had a satisfying love life, she felt their intimacy lacked the love and trust two people have for each other. She was afraid of getting hurt. If Don left her, the way every other person in her life had, she didn't know what she would do.

One evening he showed up after work, looking more pensive than usual. As she poured him a cup of tea he said "Emily, I found Jenn today."

"Where? Is she O K.? Is she coming home?"

"I picked her up off the street, by the High Lighter Hotel. She looks like hell to be honest. Once she got into the car she recognized me. I promised I wasn't going to arrest her; I just wanted to see how she was doing. She was pretty strung out, but was on her way to the inner city youth shelter by St, James church. I know the place. The girls go there for medical advice, shelter from abuse, food, and clean clothes, whatever they need. She begged me to bring her home, but I refused.

"You refused. What on earth were you thinking? You know I want her here."

"Emily, I told her the only way I would take her home to you was if she was clean and sober. If she wanted to go that way, I would find a place for her at Amber House. All she had to do was let me know. I gave her my card with my private cell phone number on it."

Emily was enraged. "Who the hell do you think you are to tell my daughter something like that? She is my daughter, and you don't have any right to say that to her."

"I did it for you. I don't want her walking in here taking advantage and upsetting you again."

Emily was angry beyond words, "Don't you ever presume to speak for me again. That is my decision, not yours. This is her home, and these doors will always be open to her."

"Go ahead, let her steal you blind, but don't come crying on my shoulder when she does. Seems to me like going to those meetings is a waste of time, you haven't learned a damn thing." Don retorted.

One angry word led to another. They were both frustrated and taking out their frustration on each other. Then Don stopped arguing. He took a long look at Emily and said "I don't need this in my life." He walked out, slamming the door behind him muttering she *has too many problems for me. I should have known better than to get involved with her in the first place. This will never work, and I am going to get out while the getting is good."*

He admonished himself for breaking his one rule – don't get involved. He wasn't going back into that house, even though he knew walking away was going to hurt for a long time.

The instant the door slammed Emily made a choice. She couldn't bear the thought of Don not being a part of her life. Her love for Jenn would never change, but she couldn't let him leave.

She opened the front door, ran down the sidewalk and caught up to him as he was getting in to his car. "Don wait, don't go. I'm sorry."

He stopped, turned, opened his arms and she ran into them. They stood there for a long time. Then taking him by the hand, she led him to the bench under the maple tree.

Don apologized. "You are right Emily. It wasn't my place to give her that ultimatum. It would have been better if I had just been another cop, checking on her welfare. I couldn't stand the thought you hurting more than you do now."

"You are right, it wasn't your place, but I understand why you did it. You were protecting me by making sure my daughter was safe. That and you knew it was the only way she could come home. She needed to hear those words from someone other than me."

They sat on the bench for a long time holding hands, murmuring in low voices. In the end they agreed to disagree about Jenn. He promised he would keep an eye out for her on a professional level, and she agreed to back the ultimatum he had given her daughter to the best of her ability. Both of them realized that there may come a time when she wouldn't be able to keep her promise. They would handle that, if and when, they had to.

As Don was preparing to leave, Emily stood up, put both hands on his shoulders and said, "Next to Jenn, you are the most important person in my life. I can't imagine not having you in it. I am falling in love with you Don Beatty, and I don't want to."

When he opened his mouth to say something, she touched her finger to his lips, "Go home," she said, "don't say anything."

As he was driving away from the house he said out loud. *Emily Stuart, you had me from the first time we met. I wonder if your ex-husband will ever realize what he gave up.*

Three evenings later, when she returned from her AHPCAD meeting there was a message on her phone. It was from Jenn.

"Mom, please come and get me. I am in jail. I have been arrested for prostitution, but they have it all wrong. Please don't leave me here. I promise to do everything you tell me this time. I love you."

Emily erased the message, and then phoned Elsie. This time she was going to let Jenn stay where she was. Elsie arrived within minutes, and listened patiently as Emily berated herself about being a poor wife, and an even poorer mother. The only words of encouragement she offered to Emily were, "you are doing the right thing."

Don kept her informed. Jenn was given thirty days in jail and Emily was relieved. At least she would know where she was going to be for the next little while.

She went to visit Jenn while she was in jail, but their meeting was unsatisfactory for both of them. Jenn was mad at her and refused to go home when she was out. She did promise to call her mother once a week. For the first few weeks, after she was released, Jenn phoned every Sunday evening. Then the calls stopped. When she tried to call Jenn's cell phone she was informed that the number was no longer in service.

Once again Emily went looking for her daughter. Carrying her last school picture in her pocket, she walked the streets of the East side.

She approached the many groups of women standing on the sidewalk; showed them the picture, explained that her daughter had just turned seventeen, and that she wanted to take her home. Those that did recognize her hadn't seen her for a long time. Finally one of the older women said, "Honey. Go to St. James church. They have a drop-in center there and a lot of the girls go there. Maybe they know where she is. If you go now they should still be open."

The next evening, as soon as she was off work, she drove directly to the drop-in center. In the daylight the street was not as sinister as it appeared after dark. As soon as she walked in the door an older gray haired lady came over and said, "May I help you? I am Samantha Adams, the director."

"I am Emily Stuart. I am looking for my daughter. Have you seen this girl?" she asked showing her Jenn's picture.

"Oh, that's Jennie. She comes in here quite often, but she hasn't been around for a while." Then she waved to a tall, raven haired girl. "Sunshine, come over here, for a minute."

The young girl sauntered over and Mrs. Adams said, "This is Jennie's mother, and she is trying to find her. Have you seen or heard from her lately? I know the two of you are tight at times."

"I haven't seen her for a couple of weeks." Sunshine replied, "She's jail bait, and the last I heard was that Skeeter took her out of town until things cooled down. Too many cops know who she is, and every time she gets arrested cuts into his profits."

"Why would he do that?" Emily asked.

"She looks like a child, is cute, and should be in school, not here with us. Even though she was wasted most of the time, she made him a lot of money. Some of those creeps like them young."

Instantly Emily felt sick to her stomach. This was her daughter Sunshine was talking about.

Reaching into her purse and taking out a pen and piece of paper she wrote down her cell phone number, gave one copy to Sunshine, the other to Samantha. "If she shows up, please call me, but don't tell her you did. All I want to do is talk with her."

"Good luck with that." Sunshine replied. "Skeeter was pretty upset when you put her in rehab. That cost him a fortune, and Jennie has been trying to make it up on her back ever since. Poor kid." Sunshine looked at her watch, "time to go. I'll be sure to call if I hear anything,"

Emily was shaken by what Sunshine had told her. *What kind of a man does this to young girls? Does this go on all the time, and why haven't the police put a stop to it?*

After that evening, Emily felt compelled to help the girls on the street. They had nobody to stand up for them. Most of them were caught up in terrible situations and had no way out. The one thing she noticed the most was that they didn't have a safe place to turn to, other than the drop-in center. Each day when they left, they were at the mercy of the streets again.

Every other day, as soon as she was off work, she returned to the drop-in center. She passed around sandwiches and coffee. Sometimes she drove the girls to the hospital when they were sick, or had been beat up. Other times she dug through the piles of donated clothing to find decent warm clothing for them to wear. The women came to trust her and opened up to her.

She listened to their stories. Each one of them was like driving a nail into her heart. Still, Jenn had not shown up, and nobody seemed to know where she was. The word on the street was that she was still out of town.

One evening, after all of the girls had left, she and Samantha started talking. Emily related her story, and then said, "I can't for the life of me understand how this happened. She had everything she needed, was the top of her class, and popular. She was planning to go to college. I know what happened to her father affected her, I just didn't realize how much."

Samantha replied, "There was nothing you could have done once Skeeter got his hooks into her. These guys look for girls who are young and vulnerable. They pay attention to them. They buy them pretty things, and convince them that they are in love with them. The girl is flattered by all of the attention she is getting from an older man. Once she trusts him, things change. These guys then demand payment for all of the money they have spent. They force them into submission either by beating them, or giving them drugs. Either way the girl feels that she has no choice. She is too embarrassed to call her parents, so in order to pay back the money she owes she does what he demands. If she resists or tries to run away it's even worse. You don't want to hear what some of these girls have been forced into doing. They have nobody to turn to.

I personally know of one young girl who tried to run away from Skeeter. He tied her to a bed, and then served her up to his friends at a party. She was never the same after that. She was only fourteen years old."

"What happened to her?" Emily felt sick to her stomach.

"She died of a drug over dose last fall." Samantha quietly replied. "Believe me, Skeeter is an expert at this. He usually runs three or four girls at a time, and if it gets too hot, he takes them out of town until things cool off. When they are of no more value to him, he sells them to another pimp."

"What does that mean?"

"Skeeter takes better care of his girls than some. There are a few who are sadistic –you should see what they do to those poor girls. What we need is a shelter they can go to and be safe, one that offers a chance to turn their lives around."

"Do you think that is what has happened to my daughter?"

"Jennie uses drugs to cover up her pain. If Skeeter thinks she is getting out of line, he cuts off her drug supply. She feels she has no choice but to work for him. Quite frankly, I think she can't find a way out, and has given up. She probably doesn't care anymore. The idea of living without drugs scares her more than what she has to do every day."

Late one night Emily's ringing cell phone woke her up. "It's me, Sunshine. Jennie is back."

"Ask her to call me. I need to know for myself."

Hours later her phone rang again. "Mom, it's me."

"Honey, are you okay? Do you want me to come and get you? I can be there in five minutes. If not me, then go to Samantha or call Don Beatty. One of us will come right away."

"I am fine. Mom, I love you. I am sorry. Please don't hate me?"

"Jenn, I love you, and I have never stopped. When you are ready, I will make sure you get the help you need. I will never hate you."

"I know. I'll try and call you again in a few days. Skeeter took my phone away, so I am using Sunshine's. I can't let him know I have talked to you."

A week later, there was a pounding on her front door. Before she could open it, a tall burly man forced his way in. He had a gun in his hand, and was wearing a black leather jacket with a crest on the back of it. "Where is that conniving little bitch Jennie?" he screamed at her.

"I don't know. I haven't seen her for months. Who are you? If you don't get out right now I am going to call the police." Emily was terrified.

"Don't lie to me," he yelled, pushing her up against the wall, his hand gripping her throat. "Tell me where that little bitch is. Skeeter told me I could trust her that I would have nothing to worry about. I gave her 10,000 dollars to pick up a package for me five days ago, and nobody has seen her since. If she has run off with my money I will kill her."

"I don't know," Emily gasped as his hand chocked her. She was finding it hard to breathe, and was very afraid for herself and for her daughter. This man seemed to be capable of anything.

Then he released his grip on her throat, pulled back his hand and slapped her across the face as hard as he could. "You tell her I am looking for her; name is Black Jack. She knows who I am and where to find me. Nobody screws with me and gets away with it. She and Skeeter are going to pay for messing with me." He threw Emily to the floor, and left, slamming the door behind him.

Her face stung from where he slapped her and her throat hurt from the pressure he put on it. She lay there on the floor shaking like a leaf, until she was sure he was gone. Then staggering to her feet she locked the door behind him.

Oh Jenn, what have you done? What have you got yourself into?

Still shaking, she phoned Don. When he answered she started to cry.

"Emily what is it? What's wrong?"

"A man was here looking for Jenn. He had a gun. He slapped me. He...."

"I am on my way." he said, "lock your doors and don't let anyone in."

After he arrived, he convinced her to file assault charges. He knew who Black Jack was and where he could be found. "We will pick him up, and that will get him off the street long enough for us to find Jenn and get her to a safe place. Skeeter deserves whatever he gets"

Emily was sick with worry. The police caught up with Skeeter, and arrested him for living off the avails of prostitution and rape, because Jenn was still a minor, but both Jenn and Black Jack were nowhere to be found. Don promised to keep looking.

Ten days later, when Emily arrived home from work she sensed something was different. Usually she used the front door, but today she had stopped at the Hardware store and bought two new chairs for the deck. That was the only reason she went to the back of the house. Immediately she saw that the back door had been forced open. Then she remembered she had forgotten to set the alarm that morning.

She stood there feeling afraid and confused about going into the house until she saw Jenn's face peeking out from behind the kitchen curtains. Emily looked around to make sure she was alone, and then went in. Emily was shocked at her daughter's appearance. She looked worse than the last time she had seen her.

"Mom, I'm in big trouble." Jenn said.

"I know. That Black Jack guy was here looking for you."

"I have to get away. I can't stay here anymore. If he finds me, I am as good as dead. Skeeter is in jail, he can't protect me from there."

"Jenn let me make you something to eat. I'll phone Don, and we will find a safe place for you. First, tell me what this is all about."

"Skeeter gave me Black Jack's money to go pick up a shipment of drugs that was coming in. I was high, and Tony, the guy I was to meet, suggested we should try them first – you know to make sure they were good.

We stayed at Tony's place for a while at the edge of town until we used up all the drugs he had brought, and then used Black Jack's money to buy more. It was a stupid thing to do, and now I am in bad trouble. I have to get away as soon as I can. Can you give me some money so I can get a bus ticket?"

Against her better judgment, Emily went into her purse and handed Jenn one hundred and fifty dollars. "This is all I have. This should be enough to buy a bus ticket out of town. When you let me know where you are, I'll send you some more."

"That's okay mom, this is enough. As soon as I find a place I promise to let you know where I am. Sunshine will know too. Love you mom," and then she was gone. That was the last time Emily saw her daughter alive. Later Elsie's words would haunt her. "Never give her money; she will use it for something else."

CHAPTER TWENTY

In her mind, Emily struggled to accept the eventuality that one day the drugs may claim her daughter's life. She knew one day her biggest fear was going to become a fact, but she had to keep trying everything in her power to prevent this from happening. It was out of her hands now. The only way Jenn could come out of this was to give up the drugs on her own and fight her demons to recover. If, and when, Jenn chose this route, she would be there for her daughter one hundred percent.

Even though she was expecting this day to come, when it actually did, she realized a person isn't really prepared. The morning Don phoned her she actually felt her heart break into two pieces.

"Emily," Don Beatty said softly. "I have some bad news for you. One of the officers found Jennifer this morning lying in an alley off Crawford Street. I am on my way to pick you up and take you to the hospital."

Emily didn't say a word on the phone. All she could think was *Please God, not yet. Not yet.* Quickly she ran into her room and dressed in a pair of jeans and t-shirt that she snatched from the closet. She didn't even stop to comb her hair. On her way out the door, she grabbed her purse and black ultra-suede jacket from the front hall closet, and waited on the front porch. When Don drove up in a police car, she ran to the car and they left blue lights flashing and siren wailing. Later she couldn't remember how she got to the hospital.

"Where is she?" Emily demanded.

"County General I.C.U. Prepare yourself. She is unconscious, and in bad shape. Whoever beat her up did a real number on her. I have spoken with the doctor, but he isn't saying much."

"Are they sure it is her? Maybe it's another girl?"

"It's her, Emily. Tucked into the back corner of her purse was a note with your name and number to call in an emergency."

"Don, we both know who did this," she stated. "It has to be that Black Jack guy, you know the one who came to my house that day. He said he would get even with her."

"Yes, I'm sure he is the one who did this. I promise you Emily that I will get to the bottom of this, and nail the creep responsible."

Ten minutes later they pulled up in front of the Emergency doors of the County General hospital. Emily jumped out of the car and ran down the hall way to the admitting station. "What floor is I C U on?"

"Six," replied the clerk, not looking up from the computer screen in front of her, "Elevators to your left."

Emily ran into the first open elevator, and began frantically pushing the number six button. Finally the doors closed, and, after what seemed an eternity, opened on the sixth floor.

Gathering her strength and trying to appear as calm as possible, she walked up to the nursing station and said, "I am Emily Stuart, my daughter Jennifer has been admitted here."

"Come with me Mrs. Stuart," one of the nurses said kindly. They stopped in front of a curtained off cubicle, and the nurse tried to warn her. "Mrs. Stuart you need to prepare yourself before you go in. Your daughter is in critical condition, and we are doing everything we can for her. This is bed twelve. You go ahead, and I will tell the doctor you are here. He wants to talk with you."

Emily gasped when she pulled the curtain aside and saw her daughter lying there. Her Jenn, once so full of life, was an emaciated skeleton, barely making a bump under the blankets covering her. Her face was black and blue. There was a cast on her right wrist, and tubes going in and out of her body. She was hooked to a monitor, and on the I V pole a bottle of blood was slowly dripping into her arm.

She stood frozen to the spot. Part of her wanted to run away, to refuse to recognize that this was her daughter lying in the bed. The other part of her knew that she would be there for as long as she was needed.

"Mrs. Stuart?" a voice from behind her broke the silence, "I am Dr. Pike." He was a young man about Emily's age. "Please step out here so we can talk."

"How is she?" Emily asked woodenly, trying to keep her emotions in check.

"The next twenty four hours are critical. We did an emergency operation to remove her spleen and stop the internal bleeding. As well, we have a drain in her skull to relieve the pressure from the bleeding there. We are sure she was repeatedly kicked in the head and abdomen, and as a result has fourteen broken ribs and a fractured skull. We are unable to determine yet whether or not she has suffered any brain damage.

The fact that she is malnourished and dependent upon drugs is complicating her recovery. We are keeping her heavily sedated to relieve the withdrawal symptoms her body is going through. This also keeps her from thrashing around and increasing the pressure in her skull. You can stay with her for as long as you like, and we will let you know immediately if there is any change in her condition.

Emily sighed wearily, "thank you doctor."

Then she turned, went back into the cubicle and walked directly to her daughter's side. Taking Jenn's small hand in hers she said, "Hi Jenn, it's mom, I'm here with you. Nobody is ever going to hurt you again, and I am not leaving your side until you are ready to come home. Baby, you have to fight to stay with us. I love you, please try and stay with me."

A hand gently touched her shoulder. "It's me Emily, I brought you a chair." said Don.

She looked up at him and smiled gratefully putting her other hand on top of his. "Thank you. I am going to stay here with her for as long as she needs me."

"What does the doctor say?"

"That the next twenty four hours are critical, and that they are doing all they can for her. She has a fractured skull, broken ribs, and they had to remove her spleen."

He kissed the top of Emily's head, and then gave her shoulder a squeeze. "I'll be off duty in a couple of hours. I'll come back then."

She shook her head in agreement. As he left the cubicle, he wiped a tear from his eye. This case was really getting to him. He was determined to catch the so and so, and everyone else who had mistreated this child. If he ever got the chance, he would like to give them a taste of their own medicine.

Emily stayed by her daughter's bed side throughout the long day and night, never letting go of her hand. She talked to her, reminded her of all the good times they had as a family, the things she had done as a child, and the happy times when her dad was with them. She reminded her of the silly things they had done together, like walking outside in the rain in their bare feet. She sang to her, but she didn't cry. She tried to pour her own strength into her daughter - urging her to fight, to stay with her.

The staff was excellent; they brought her a coffee and sandwiches, all of which went untouched. The first time she dozed off, dropping her head on Jenn's bed, someone had put a blanket around her shoulders.

Don came and stayed with her for a while. "Emily," he said, "take a break. I'll stay with her."

"What if she wakes up and I'm not here?"

"Emily, I promise I will find you right away."

"No, I am going to stay here." Don didn't argue with her. He could see the pain and determination etched in her face.

Emily looked up at him sadly, "you know, finding the guy who did this isn't going to change what happened. Somehow we have to find a way to save the girls that kind of scum preys upon." Motioning her hand to her daughter she said, "My daughter didn't deserve this. She was a good girl and had much to offer the world. We have to find a way to stop this from happening over and over to other girls."

Throughout the next night, and into the early morning the nurses were encouraged by the improvement in Jenn's condition. When Dr. Pike returned he reported, "She is stable and improving slowly. We are going to begin to lighten her sedation, let her become more aware and see how she responds. If she gets too restless, we will have to increase it again."

Hours later, she felt the grip of Jenn's fingers tighten on her hand. When she looked into her daughter's eyes, a tear was coursing from the corner of her eye making its way down her cheek.

"Don't cry Jenn. I am here, and I am not leaving. If you can hear me, squeeze my hand again. I love you. I'm not mad at you. Together we will get through this, I promise."

A brief smile touched Jenn's lips, and then alarms began ringing from all of the machines. The nurses came running in, one pushing a crash cart. Emily looked at the monitor and, now there was a flat line where only seconds ago there had been a heartbeat.

She put out her hand to stop the nurses. "Leave her be. Finally she is at peace. Nothing or nobody can hurt her anymore."

"Mrs. Stuart, are you sure this is what you want? We only have a few minutes."

"Yes. She is not suffering now."

She wrapped her arms around her daughter and rocked her back and forth like she had done when she had a nightmare. Then she sat there holding Jenn's lifeless hand as long as they would let her. She signed the forms stating that she had refused resuscitation efforts for her daughter. Dr. Pike came in and explained they were sure she died from a blood clot in her lungs from the broken ribs, and asked if they could do an autopsy. She also signed the papers consenting to that.

After a while, they left her alone in her grief. Every once in a while, a nurse would stick her head around the curtain to check on her, but it seemed all too soon that she heard Don's voice say, "Come Emily, it's time to go home."

"I know," she whispered. She kissed her daughter on the cheek, and replaced a strand of hair that was out of place. She was grateful the nurses had removed all of the equipment and beeping monitors from her body. She tucked her daughter's hand under the sheets and straightened them one last time, then she collapsed into Don's open arms sobbing. He put his arm around her and gently guided her out of the room.

CHAPTER TWENTY ONE

Emily was grief stricken. Repeatedly she questioned herself *did I do the right thing? Should I have at least let them try to resuscitate her? What if they had been able to bring her back? Would I still have her?* Common sense told her that she had made the right decision. She knew that, but the "what if" questions kept haunting her.

Don took charge. He made all of the arrangements according to Emily's wishes. He notified the funeral home, arranged for a grave side service, and contacted the facility where Ben was imprisoned. He spoke to the chaplain who promised to relay the sad message to Ben. He was also able to make arrangements with the authorities for Ben to attend his daughter's funeral

On a cold, fall, rainy day, on the day of her eighteenth birthday, Jennifer Stuart was laid to rest. Few people attended the service – Ben, herself, Sunshine, Elsie, Mrs. Pomery and Don. As Jenn's casket was lowered into the ground Emily placed a rose on top and stood there watching as it disappeared.

She walked over and put her arms around Ben to comfort him. His eyes were red from crying and he was visibly shaken. There was no room left for anger in Emily's heart

"This is my fault," he said. "Can you ever forgive me? I did this to you and Jenn. I am so sorry."

"No Ben, this is just the way it was supposed to be. You made your choices, and so did Jenn. Nobody knew this would be the final result. Now you need to forgive yourself in order to move on. I forgave you a long time ago. I will always love both of you." She kissed him lightly on the cheek, hugged him, and then walked back to her daughter's grave.

Before the guard led Ben away, he asked to speak to Don. They spoke for a few minutes and then Ben and the guard left. He walked away a broken man.

Don let Emily stand by her daughter's grave for a long time. Finally he put his arm around her and said, "Come Emily, let's go home. There is nothing more we can do here."

He led her to the car and got her settled in the front seat. As soon as he got into the driver's side, she turned to him and asked, "What did Ben say to you?"

"He asked if we were together, and I said yes. He told me to love and treasure you, and that the two of you were the best things that ever happened to him. I promised I would forever, if you will have me. I love you Emily Stuart."

Through her tears she replied, "I don't know how to go on from here. I wouldn't have had the strength to get through this without you. Thank you for all you have done, but I have one more thing to ask you."

"What's that Emily?"

She reached over and put her hand on top of his. "Do you think you could take me home and stay with me? I don't want to be alone right now."

He turned and looked at her. "Are you sure that's what you want? I could get Elsie to come over."

"Yes," she replied. " I don't want anybody else except you."

The next day an announcement appeared in two newspapers, the local one, the other in the town where they used to live.

"On the day of her eighteenth birthday Jennifer Elaine Stuart was laid to rest, her long battle with drug addiction over. For those who wish to donate, they may do so to the Jennifer Stuart Rescue fund in care of Amber House. All donations will be used exclusively for rescuing young women from the streets, and supporting them in their battle against substance abuse"

Every child to has the right to live free and unafraid.

Mother of four and grandmother of four boys Judy lives with her husband Bob, and their five year old Shih Tzu named Missy Sue in Grimshaw Ab.

Judy began writing at an early age, but it wasn't until she retired from the business world that she was able to follow her passion for writing, and give voice to her dream of empowering women.

Judy's books are being sold internationally in the UK and USA.

You may contact her at:: jcoates@telusplanet.net